"I'm so sorry. I didn't realize someone was sitting here."

Dark eyes looked up at him. There was a flare of annoyance, and then her gaze narrowed.

"*You,*" she said accusingly. "Do you always ski like some flash idiot?"

The thick Scottish accent slayed him as pieces started to drop into place—it was the woman from last night.

"Do you always hire a driver that drives like an idiot?"

Her mouth fell open.

He smiled at her spark and sass. He leaned over and held out his hand. "Stefan."

She eyed his hand before shaking it firmly. "Paige."

"Where are you from in Scotland, Paige?"

"Oh no. You don't get to sit down all smug after, (a)," she counted on her fingers, "you tried to blame us for a car accident last night, (b) you tried to drown me in snow with your flashy and unsafe stop earlier and (c) you just bulldozed past me and spilled my coffee." She pointed to the table in front of her. "If you'd knocked my toast, it would have been game over."

He laughed. "Is there anything you don't want to blame me for?"

She looked at her half-filled coffee cup. "Nope, I think everything is absolutely your fault."

Dear Reader,

I am the biggest Christmas fan and writing a Christmas story is always my favorite thing in the world. This one has a real hint of serious stuff as my heroine, Paige McLeod, is contemplating leaving the job she no longer loves. This is the reality for many staff in the NHS, most of whom are exhausted and feel as if they have no more to give. I hope I've handled it sensitively. I've given her a Swiss hero in Stefan Bachman, the busiest man on the planet, because he doesn't want to stop and take time to contemplate the guilt he's been left with. Being snowed in together makes Paige and Stefan face their demons, but also gives them the time to fall in love!

Hope you enjoy!

Love,

Scarlet

SNOWED IN WITH THE SURGEON

SCARLET WILSON

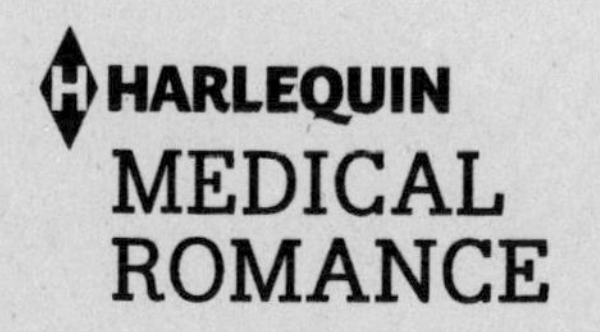

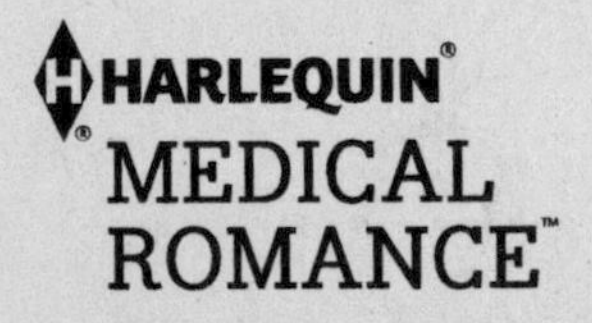

ISBN-13: 978-1-335-73752-6

Snowed In with the Surgeon

For questions and comments about the quality of this book, please contact us at CustomerService@Harlequin.com.

Harlequin Enterprises ULC
22 Adelaide St. West, 41st Floor
Toronto, Ontario M5H 4E3, Canada
www.Harlequin.com

Printed in U.S.A.

Scarlet Wilson wrote her first story aged eight and has never stopped. She's worked in the health service for twenty years, having trained as a nurse and a health visitor. Scarlet now works in public health and lives on the west coast of Scotland with her fiancé and their two sons. Writing medical romances and contemporary romances is a dream come true for her.

Books by Scarlet Wilson

Harlequin Medical Romance

Night Shift in Barcelona

The Night They Never Forgot

Neonatal Nurses

Neonatal Doc on Her Doorstep

The Christmas Project

A Festive Fling in Stockholm

Double Miracle at St. Nicolino's Hospital

Reawakened by the Italian Surgeon

His Blind Date Bride
Marriage Miracle in Emergency

Visit the Author Profile page
at Harlequin.com for more titles.

To all the people who love Christmas and
Christmas movies just as much as I do.
And to the new member of the family:
Max, the best red Labrador in the world!

Praise for
Scarlet Wilson

"[Charming] and oh so passionate, *Cinderella and the Surgeon* was everything I love about Harlequin Medicals. Author Scarlet Wilson created a flowing story rich with flawed but likable characters and… will be sure to delight readers and have them sighing happily with that sweet ending."

—*Harlequin Junkie*

Scarlet Wilson won the 2017 RoNA Rose Award
for her book
Christmas in the Boss's Castle

PROLOGUE

IT HAPPENED IN a flash. One second Paige McLeod was on her feet, the next she was flying into a wall, smashing against it and landing on the floor.

For a few seconds her brain didn't really compute what had happened. A&E was crazily busy—had been for the last few hours. The waiting room was packed, every cubicle full, and two ambulances were still waiting to offload their patients in the receiving bay.

She tried to breathe, and immediately realised her mistake. The air had been knocked clean out of her. Trying to breathe was a limited possibility. Her hand went to the back of her head, rubbing the spot that had hit the wall.

She was surrounded by feet, familiar voices, shouts and a scramble on the floor next to her.

Leo's face appeared in front of her. He

muttered an expletive as he grabbed her around the shoulders and leaned over her, clearly doing a quick assessment.

'Paige? Are you okay?'

She could already feel his assessing eyes on her body. He looked over his shoulder to one of the black-uniformed cops—a familiar presence in a Scottish A&E on a Saturday night. 'Have you got him?'

There was an affirmative nod. Leo sighed and concentrated his gaze on Paige. 'Come on, let's get you checked.' He helped her to her feet.

She started to shake her head. 'It's too busy—' Then stopped as a wave of nausea surged upwards. She put her hand to her mouth as Leo steered her into the nearest sluice room and pulled her hair back from her face as she was sick. His muttered expletives told her just how angry he was.

Then there was another. 'You're bleeding,' he said.

She lifted her hand to her head and pulled it back. Sure enough, her fingers were smeared with blood. Before she had a chance to speak she felt something pressed against her head. Leo had her in a cubicle, a quick clean of her head wound and some paper sutures applied.

She was only glad he hadn't had to shave part of her scalp in order to put some proper stitches in. The wound must be superficial. It would be okay.

A few minutes later she was seated in the comfortable chair behind his desk, a glass of water in one hand, a sick bowl on the desk, as he shone a pen torch in her eyes.

She sighed and leaned back in the chair. 'I'm fine, I'm fine. I'll get back out there in a minute.'

'No, you won't.'

She blinked. She'd been struggling recently but hadn't spoken about it, and didn't really want anyone to know. She thought she'd kept her feelings hidden. But maybe she hadn't fooled Leo.

The comfortable chair didn't feel quite so comfy. She sat up. 'What do you mean?'

He let out a huge sigh and settled in the hard chair opposite. She'd never really thought about it before, but Leo's chair was immensely comfortable, and the chair at the other side of the desk was hard and unyielding—almost as if he didn't want any guest to stay too long. Clever guy. He'd been the head of this Glasgow A&E for as long as anyone could remember. There was a lot to learn here.

His voice was deep. 'Paige, this is the third time you've been assaulted at work in six months. Last time with your head injury I…' His voice cracked.

She leaned towards him and put her hand over his. 'That was *not* your fault.'

Leo lowered his head for a few seconds. Everyone knew the punch that had caused Paige's head injury had been aimed at Leo. For an older guy he was light on his feet and had ducked sideways to avoid it, not realising Paige was directly behind him.

His dark grey eyes looked at her. There was an air of resignation about him. 'Attacks on NHS staff are increasing. We both know that. And they're entirely unacceptable. We all know A&E bears the brunt of this. We have the drunks. The confused. The upset, and the angry. You're a brilliant doctor, Paige. I don't want to lose you. But I also don't want you to accept this as part of your job. None of us should.'

Paige blinked back tears that had formed in her eyes. Things were starting to catch up with her. Her ribs and shoulder were aching a little, and her head was pounding. She lifted one hand. 'But you need me. We're slammed out there.'

Leo nodded. 'We are. But I trust our colleagues. Everyone has been triaged. Those who need immediate care are getting it. Those who can wait, will wait.'

He leaned back and folded his arms. Then she watched him swallow. Oh, no. This was serious.

She was panicking inside. Those words. *I don't want to lose you.* It was as if he'd reached inside her head and seen all the thoughts she'd been having. Her feelings of self-doubt. The early mornings her alarm had gone off and she'd woken with a sensation of dread. The near belief that the last few attacks in A&E had been because she hadn't been completely on her game, and she'd probably deserved what had happened. She'd been thinking about leaving. About handing in her notice. But it made her feel like such a failure. Six years of university, followed by six years of working as a doctor. What an absolute waste. Didn't everyone want to be a doctor?

'Paige, when did you last have some time off?'

The words seemed to come out of nowhere, pulling her back from her thoughts. She blinked and pressed her lips together. She knew the answer to his question but didn't want to say it out loud. She'd willingly cancelled her first lot of annual leave when a fellow colleague had problems in her pregnancy. She'd cancelled her second lot when another colleague had come down with a short-term acute illness. It was what any reasonable human would do.

She lifted one hand. 'We're coming up on Christmas—our busiest time. I'm due to work. There's no way I can have time off right now.'

Leo gave a sad smile. 'Dr McLeod, as the head of this department, I've let you down. You've been assaulted in my department three times in six months, and you've cancelled holidays to cover for colleagues. Your dedication and expertise is not in question, Paige, but your wellbeing is.'

She opened her mouth to speak, but wasn't quite sure what to say. Now she really thought that Leo might know what she'd been thinking.

Leo continued. 'I'm giving you this week as sick leave, then four weeks as annual leave. By the time you come back, the new security staff I've requested for over a year will be in place, and our two new medics from Spain and Ireland will be in post. We'll have a full complement of staff, and we should be safer.'

She swallowed and looked around Leo's office. His walls were decorated with awards he'd been given, and photos of him with his arms around colleagues. All of the colleagues looked at him with admiration in their eyes. He was probably one of the best doctors she'd ever work with. She *was* tired. She was feeling a bit jaded. And all she really wanted to do was curl up in her bed. She was so used to clocking in every day, of doing extra hours to ensure that an elderly patient got a bed in the ward they needed, or waiting for a set of blood results or X-ray to come through so she could finish her care.

She knew exactly what she was doing. It was easy to push the memories of the assaults from her brain and stick them in some kind of box where they could be hidden and ignored. No member of healthcare staff should be assaulted. The whole world believed that. But it *did* happen. And Leo was right. It was time to take stock and ask questions. That was why he was in the job.

She looked down. Her hands were shaking. She hadn't even realised. Her voice shook too. 'What will I do?' she asked.

Work was her life and that was part of the reason she was so scared about the thoughts that had been circulating in her brain. If she didn't have her work, what would she have left? Her family was scattered across the country. Her close friends were all in the health service. All would be working over the next few weeks. She had a very nice flat, but lived alone. She didn't want to be alone right now.

Something flickered across Leo's eyes. 'You ski, don't you?'

She nodded. Paige had always been a sporty kind of girl, and had skied in a number of resorts around the world.

Leo flipped open his laptop and made a few keystrokes. He spun the laptop around. 'What do you think of this place?'

Paige's eyes widened. It was like a scene from a film. A snow-set chalet with large windows, perched on a hillside somewhere.

'It…it's magnificent,' she said simply. 'Where is it?'

Leo nodded. 'Switzerland. It belongs to a friend. He loans it out frequently. Usually to medical staff, or people who need some respite. It's right next to a ski resort. Perfect for you, really. Let me check the dates with him.' He tapped furiously.

Paige frowned. 'What?'

Leo waved his hand. 'You can go.' Then

he looked up, and frowned. 'Do you have other plans? Am I overstepping?'

She shook her head as tears welled in her eyes. 'No, I don't have other plans. But... how much is it?'

She hadn't been skiing in two years. She would absolutely love to go, and had never skied in Switzerland before.

Leo smiled at her. 'It's free. You just have to arrange your flights. My friend—he's a baron, an inventor—you might have heard of him. He's usually getting maligned in the press somewhere. His more philanthropic efforts always go unnoticed, but he actually likes that. He doesn't want the world to know he has a whole host of houses around the world that he loans out for people who need them.' Leo shook his head. 'He prefers his more cut-throat image. Helps with business apparently.'

'I don't know,' she said hesitantly. This whole thing was swamping her and her head was starting to pound uncomfortably, just like her shoulder. Part of her wondered if this was some kind of dream. Or a result of the head knock. Maybe she was actually still lying on the floor outside?

Leo's brow wrinkled. 'I mean, would you

prefer New York, Bermuda, Hawaii, Gibraltar, or maybe South Africa or Brazil?'

Paige's eyes widened. 'He has houses in all those places?'

Leo rested his hands in his lap. 'He has more. And it makes him sound frivolous. But this is what he does with those houses. A large number of charitable organisations use them for their clients too. The only condition is that it's kept quiet. He doesn't want journalists swooping in and invading the privacy of those who need it.' Leo looked thoughtful. 'It's been going on for more than twenty years.' He gave a shrug. 'I just thought the skiing place would suit you best.'

She nodded just as there was a ping from Leo's computer.

His face broke into a wide grin. 'Ah, there we are. It's free.'

'He's got back to you already?'

Leo laughed. 'I told you, he's a businessman. He uses every tool available. There's an automatic confirmation booking system for these places. It's yours.'

He pushed his laptop towards Paige again. 'Take a better look and I'll send the details to your phone.'

She really couldn't believe this. One minute she was being knocked against a wall at work, the next, she had five weeks off and was heading to some unnamed resort in the Alps where she could ski all day and sleep in what looked like a luxury chalet at night.

She sagged back in the chair.

'I need to observe you for the next six hours.' Leo's words were said as some kind of aside.

She shook her head and held out her hand. 'No. Give me some of the paracetamol I know you have in your top desk drawer. Check my pupils again if you want. I just had an unexpected knock.'

'You vomited,' he said again sharply, his doctor's eyes narrowed.

'Autonomic reaction,' she replied, equally sharply. 'And Esther is off today. I can speak to her if I feel unwell.'

Leo kept his gaze firmly on her as he pulled his phone from his pocket. Esther Cohen was her next-door neighbour and a fellow medic at the hospital. They had a reciprocal arrangement, with both having keys to each other's flats in case of emergency.

He finally looked down, pressed a few keys and sighed. 'Okay, I've texted her. Asked her to check on you in a few hours.'

She might have known he would have had Esther's number.

He pulled the painkillers from the desk drawer and tossed them towards her and she took two with the water she had. Her phone pinged and she looked down. All the details of the resort, along with details of the nearest airport.

'Text me when you arrive,' Leo said, coming around the desk and shining a pen torch in her eyes again, then nodding in satisfaction. 'Equal and reacting.'

He put a hand on her shoulder. 'How are you feeling? I was being serious. I can put you round in the Combined Assessment Unit for a few hours.'

This was actually real. It wasn't some weird kind of daydream. She was actually being sent home.

Paige stood up, her legs feeling less wobbly now. 'No, I'm good. I'll just grab my things from my locker.'

Leo nodded and held the door open for her. The corridor outside was a complete and utter rabble. Loud noises, shouts for assistance, staff hurrying past.

The temptation to step back into it was strong. Like a heavy commitment hanging over her head. But Leo's voice was right at her side. 'Go home, Paige,' he said quietly.

She pressed her lips together and strode

along to the changing room, grabbing her thick winter coat and swapping her light shoes for winter boots.

A few moments later she was outside. It was still dark. A few ambulance personnel nodded at her as she zipped up her coat against the immediate chill in the air. Her breath steamed in front of her.

She took a few steps away from the main entrance, moving towards the orange-tinged streetlights and her home, which was only five minutes' walk away.

As the noise dimmed behind her and flakes of snow settled on her cheeks, the tears she had been holding back for months finally started to fall.

CHAPTER ONE

STEFAN BACHMANN MOVED quickly around the empty building, trying to hide his rage. The contractor could barely keep up with his long strides.

'What about those other rooms—when are they due to be finished? And why is there still equipment missing?'

The private hospital was due to open in less than two weeks. There was no chance of that happening.

'We've had some delays,' murmured the contractor, uttering the same words he had for the last few weeks. 'Seven of the suites are finished. Electricity and water are on in one half of the building. Tiling and bathroom fittings for those seven rooms and the staff area have been completed this week. The three operating rooms and recovery area is completed—but there are a few pieces of equipment still outstanding. Kitchen is almost complete.'

It sounded reasonable. But the luxury private hospital was way behind schedule. Only half of the actual works were complete.

He walked into a large room. It was an old ward—back from when this hospital had been used in the First World War as rehabilitation for prisoners of war who were sent to recover in the mountain air.

Something curled inside his stomach. His great-grandfather had been one of those young men. Originally from Belgium, he'd been wounded and had met Stefan's great-grandmother here, one of the nurses in this hospital.

When he'd first walked through this place there had been definite echoes of the past. The hospital had been reused in what seemed like a hundred different ways since its original purpose. But this part, the place he stood in, for some reason had always remained untouched. Of course, it was in the plans to be refurbished. This was going to be the gym for the physios to use when required.

Stefan could almost laugh out loud. This whole place was going to be almost a replica of another luxury private surgery clinic he worked in just west of Hollywood. There, stars were photographed with hats on their heads and wearing sunglasses, 'pretending' to hide from the world as they attended, usually for some kind of cosmetic surgery.

This place was part of the same company. But the setting was all about privacy. The stars coming here for their surgery wouldn't want it made public. Most of them would need prolonged stays, some to recover from botched surgeries in other parts of the world, some because they needed treatment alongside their surgery. Not every star wanted the world to know they had some kind of cancer. It could affect contracts and deals for them. Stefan had a leading oncologist working alongside him. All the latest treatments were available, along with a host of highly trained staff who could administer them and monitor any after-effects.

This prestigious alpine retreat could really do some good. Which was the only reason Stefan was here. He'd been reluctant initially when he was approached about acquiring a premises in his homeland. He'd known about this old hospital all his life, and knew the site would be just what they were looking for.

It was close to an exclusive ski resort and

reached by a long, winding road which in some parts, and at some times of year, could be impassable, due to ice and snow. There were a number of private properties that lined this road, and part of the agreement for the refurbishment of the hospital was that they took on the ongoing maintenance for the road. It was obviously in the company's best interests, but it made Stefan a little uncomfortable. This road had been laughingly called 'Millionaires' Row' by the locals. The people who lived in those luxury houses were more than capable of keeping their own road in a reasonable state. But since the hospital was at the top of the track it seemed to have fallen to them.

There had already been a few issues with the building equipment—much of which was heavy. Some of the trucks had struggled in the bad weather to reach the resort, and a few had to turn back, all adding to the delays.

Stefan paused for a moment and ran his fingers through his dark hair. He wasn't even supposed to be in charge of this part of the process. He was a surgeon, not a tradesman. But their business manager was back in Hollywood, where his wife was due to have twins. He'd had to fly back, and Stefan had been left to oversee what should have been the finishing touches for the resort.

Time was something that Stefan didn't have. He'd spent his life going from one project to another, throwing himself wholeheartedly into every one of them. He'd never learned to slow down, always saying yes when asked to do extra work or take on extra responsibilities. So the fact that this project wasn't complete—that he suspected the workmen might have been taking longer than they should, felt like a personal failure.

Coming close to home amplified those feelings. When he'd told his parents he wanted to go to medical school they'd both worked day and night to help their son fulfil his dreams. They'd always had a strong work ethic and had passed that on to him.

But when he'd got a phone call from his dad to let him know his mother was sick he'd felt hideously guilty. Even worse, he'd been only halfway home when she'd died from a massive myocardial infarction.

Apparently, she'd been having occasional bouts of chest pain, but hadn't had time to see anyone. That made the guilt even worse. He had nearly completed his training at this point. He should have picked up on it. He should have intervened.

It didn't matter how many people had patted his shoulder and told him how proud his mother would have been. The sadness in his father's eyes still haunted him to this day. It made him want to work even harder, go even faster, to be worthy of the sacrifice his mother had made for him. It left him without a minute in the day, but that was the only way he could cope.

He pulled out his phone and started dictating notes. At his estimate, this place was at least six weeks behind schedule—and that was being optimistic. They couldn't open with only half the place refurbished. The front part of the building looked pristine. The suites were finished to the high standard he'd expect, with ample room for guests to have relatives or staff stay with them. But the rest of the facility was nowhere near complete.

'Do we have delivery dates for the rest of the materials?'

The contractor flicked through the paper attached to his clipboard. Stefan could tell he was stressing the man. But he knew exactly how much this had all cost. They should have been finished on time. He made a mental note to check if there were penalties included in the contract for late completion.

'Some of the materials are arriving in the next few days. There's a big delivery of minor equipment tomorrow. It should have been rescheduled until more of the works were completed but was missed.'

'What about the internet provider? That was supposed to be installed two weeks ago.'

'They had problems with the installation. They're due back tomorrow. I'll check the weather forecast, to make sure there are no problems for the rest of the deliveries.'

Stefan naturally glanced up at the sky. It was dark and gloomy. He knew that some of the tougher ski runs had been closed earlier, due to the high winds. He'd skied since he was a child and always welcomed the chance to return home and get back on the slopes. One look at the sky made him think it was highly unlikely that his favourite runs would open again later today.

He waved a hand at the contractor. 'We'll talk tomorrow. I expect all the tradesmen onsite and ready to move this project along. Enough time has been lost.'

The contractor muttered something under his breath but gave Stefan a nod as he left.

Stefan moved over to the nearest set of doors. They opened out to a balcony that had a magnificent view of the surrounding mountainside. Once the transformation was complete, this hospital would be fantastic.

He could imagine how alien this setting might have seemed to men who had been prisoners of war. A little check through history had shown there had been multiple cases of tuberculosis, amputees and those who were termed as suffering 'shellshock'. Many of the sickest had been sent here—those who were never expected to return to war. The job of the staff here had been to try to ensure the men would regain some kind of quality of life that would help them eventually return home at the end of the war. The alpine air and peaceful surroundings would have played a large part in that, just like he hoped it would assist in the recovery of the new kind of patients they would bring to this clinic.

As a plastic surgeon he could perform many of the popular procedures. He'd reshaped numerous noses, chins, abdomens, breasts and buttocks. But his passion was for the highly specialist skills required to repair babies' cleft lips and palates. He frequently spent time working for Médecins Sans Frontières on a voluntary basis, carrying out these operations all over the world.

Not all of these procedures were straightforward. Part of his agreement in his new role was to be able to bring children who required more detailed surgery to either the clinic in the US or to Switzerland for their procedure.

And even though the workload was extensive and exhausting he knew his father was proudest of the pictures he showed him of the children who could eat and speak properly because of his surgical skills. Working constantly didn't give him time or space to think about the guilt he still felt. It meant that he always had something to talk to his father about, rather than acknowledge the huge hole left in both of their lives by the death of his mother.

He gazed out over the white-topped mountains again and leaned backwards, stretching out his tense muscles. He couldn't wait to hit the slopes, but first he had to make sure everything was in order here. He had two online meetings to attend, but the internet had not yet been put into place in the hospital—another thing to add to the list. He'd have to go back down to a hotel at the base of the mountain. He'd come up here today in the hope that things might have moved on in the last two weeks. Stefan glanced at the light backpack he'd brought with him. Although the staff accommodation was ready, without internet, he couldn't function properly. He had another case of belongings in his car. He'd leave the backpack here and hope that by the time he came back up an internet connection might have been installed.

He sighed as he made his way back to his car. It was starting to get dark, and the last thing he needed was to end up driving in difficult conditions. He knew exactly what this mountain road could be like. He made another mental note to check about the activity to maintain and upgrade the road before he climbed into the car, pressed the ignition and started down the darkening road.

'Are you sure this is the way?'

Paige was trying not to appear panicked. The journey from the airport should have taken around an hour, but she'd been in this pre-booked private service car for longer than that. Whilst at first the sleek dark car had looked pristine, she'd heard the wheels spinning a few times on this road—the awfully dark road.

In her head, she'd gone from tired and weary doctor to imminent victim in some crime novel. The kind that as soon as the woman steps into a prearranged car in a foreign country, and heads down some dark country road, has the reader shaking their head in knowing anticipation of what comes next.

The driver mumbled something in reply and gave a wave of his hand. The back of the car was wide and spacious and there was a screen separating her and the driver, which made communication difficult. Her mind started to go into overdrive. She could be dumped somewhere on this mountain road. She could be left in a snowdrift. Or maybe the driver was some secret super-villain and would leave her locked in the back of the car and take off in his helicopter, leaving her to starve to death in the luxury vehicle.

She eyed the small cabinet with soda and nuts. How long would they last? She closed her eyes for a second, hearing Leo's voice in her head, telling her to calm down and give her overtired brain a rest. She'd been up for over twenty-four hours now. For some reason she couldn't sleep last night, wondering if she'd packed the right equipment, and changing her book selection several times, then making sure she had them all downloaded onto her tablet in case she lost her luggage.

Thankfully, her case and her ski equipment were in the boot of the car after being safely retrieved from the airport carousel.

There was a screech and she found herself flung to the left, cheek slamming into the side window. Her body jerked forward as the seatbelt automatically tightened and held her safely in place. The car seemed to move in slow motion, spinning sideways, then moving backwards. Lights streamed directly in front of her. But there was no sound of impact. No metal crunching.

No sensation of falling off a mountainside.

Paige took a few breaths, glad her seatbelt had limited any damage. Her shoulder might be a bit bruised, but that would be nothing new. She was about to ask the driver if he was okay when she heard a stream of angry words. The next second, the driver's door opened and he was out onto the road.

The stream of words amplified. She strained for a few moments as she struggled with the seatbelt release, trying to identify the language. She knew that four languages were spoken in Switzerland—Swiss German, French, Italian and Rhaeto-Romanic. This sounded like her first introduction to Swiss German expletives.

She gave her body a shake and stepped outside the car into the dark winding road. There was another car's headlights illuminating theirs. The brisk cold air stole her breath and she shivered.

Her driver, a short, grey-haired man, was gesturing and shouting wildly at the other guy. Whoever the other guy was, he was much taller and leaner. It was hard to see properly when the lights were directly towards her, but Paige was too tired to be polite.

She walked between the two men. 'What happened?'

For a second there was silence, probably as they both adjusted to her strong Scottish accent. When she was tired, and annoyed, her voice did tend to come across as very fierce. She took a deep breath and waved towards the two vehicles, trying to speak clearly. 'What happened? Is anyone hurt?'

The taller man turned towards her. 'Your driver doesn't seem to know how to navigate mountain roads late at night.'

He was giving her a strange look, his brow furrowed. If he wasn't quite so angry, he might be quite handsome, but being handsome wouldn't excuse his rudeness.

'Are you injured?' she asked again.

He jerked a little, as if he was just now considering other things, and replied in perfect English. 'No. Are you?'

She shook her head. 'Nothing that won't look after itself.' She folded her arms across her chest. 'Is there a reason you're causing such a scene on a dark road, in the middle of the night?'

'Me?' He looked incredulous. 'Your driver clearly doesn't know these roads. He came around that bend far too fast. He was halfway over my side of the road.'

She arched her eyebrows and glanced towards his car. It was a large four-by-four, with extremely large tyres with deep treads. It might not have snow chains, but she could bet Mr Arrogant would be able to put them on his car in an instant.

'All the more reason that a local like yourself should drive with more due care and attention—presuming, of course, that you *do* know these roads. You should be used to tourists or strangers on these roads.'

She could see the fury build behind his eyes. She knew she was being cheeky, but she didn't care. His first action hadn't been to make sure everyone was okay. His first action had been to get out of his car and shout. She tried to forget that her driver had done exactly the same.

'Idiots shouldn't be on these roads. He—' he gestured to her driver, who she was sure could follow some of the conversation, glaring at him '—shouldn't be driving at night.'

'*He* didn't have much choice, since my flight was delayed by five hours,' she countered quickly. 'And—' she looked him up and down, trying to ignore his broad shoulders, slim waist, and she definitely wasn't looking at those blue eyes she'd glimpsed as he'd turned his head in the lights '—it appears there is more than one kind of idiot on the roads tonight.'

There was silence. He stared at her for a few moments, and she wondered if the edge of his lip turned up in faint amusement. Then he shook his head. 'Are you always this friendly?'

'I was just about to ask the same.'

Silence again. 'Where are you headed—are you lost?'

Paige looked over at her driver, who had understood every word and gestured to further up the mountain road. 'I'm staying in Chalet Versailles, up the road somewhere.'

The stranger put his hands on his hips and

gave her a strange, calculating glance. Did he know who normally stayed at that lodge?

He gave a soft shake of his head again, then gestured behind him. 'It's only a few hundred metres further up on the right. The turning is clearly marked. Don't go any further. The road comes to a dead end at the hospital at the top.'

Her eyes widened and her brain sparked. 'There's a hospital up here?' She couldn't hide the surprise in her voice.

'There used to be—in the First World War, and there will be again in the future. It's not running yet.' He frowned again. 'Anyhow, if you reach that you've gone too far.'

Her stiff shoulders relaxed a little. 'See, you can be nice when you want to be.'

It was his turn to arch his eyebrows. 'Just make sure your driver takes it slowly. And warn him about driving back down the mountain. He really needs thicker tyres.'

Paige heard a distinct tut behind her, and knew instantly it was her driver. She turned back, but the stranger was already climbing back in his car. A few seconds later, he gunned the engine of his four-by-four and swept past them, leaving them in the inky-black road again.

Her driver muttered angrily and showed her back to the car, slamming the door behind her. Paige settled back into the comfortable seat. She should go back into panic mode, worrying about what might happen next. But her brain wasn't ready.

Instead, it was fixated on the tall, dark, handsome stranger. She hadn't even asked him his name. And, for some strange reason, she wished she had.

CHAPTER TWO

SHE'D NEVER BEEN this comfortable in her entire life. Last night she'd barely taken the time to look around after her still-muttering driver had dropped her off. She'd tipped him heavily in the hope it would make up for the road mishap, but had just been too tired to spend time exploring her surroundings.

She'd carried her small bag up to the bedroom at the top of the wide stairs, taken a little breath at the size of it, and promptly pulled on her pyjamas and climbed into the four-poster bed. She couldn't remember a single thing after that, but right now she could swear this was the comfiest she'd ever been.

Part of her wanted to take a note of the brand of duvet, pillows and sheets. But part of her knew it would likely all be widely outside her price range, so she just snuggled a little lower in the bed and let her eyes flicker open.

Just as she'd remembered, the room was bigger than the whole of her kitchen and living room in her flat. Most things were white. Paige cringed. She was quite accident-prone and would likely manage to cover things in coffee spills or chocolate smudges.

She pushed herself up in the bigger than king-size bed. The room was wide and inviting, a large wooden dresser, wardrobe and chest of drawers against the walls. A door leading to what she assumed was a bathroom was ajar. A television was mounted on the wall in front of her. She leaned to the side and picked up the list of instructions for all the electronics in the room. A few presses on a remote control changed the lighting from warm, to bright white, to pale pink, then violet, then green. Another button set off a low rumble. Paige watched in wonder as the blackout blind on the large window slowly lifted.

She pulled back. Bright white wasn't just in her room, it was directly outside. It was already morning and the Alps stretched in every direction, as far as the eye could see. It was like something directly from a Christmas card. White, dotted with bits of green, and a few buildings spaced out across the view.

She flung back her covers and walked over, taking a deep breath. This was absolutely gorgeous. Her overtired body was suddenly invigorated. Look at that snow! She hadn't skied in over two years and couldn't wait to get out there.

Paige stuck her feet into her slippers and washed her face, brushed her teeth and wrapped herself in the luxury bathrobe that was behind the door of her en suite bathroom.

Ten minutes later she'd toured the whole chalet. Luxurious beyond words. Seven bedrooms, all with en suite bathrooms. Two other spacious bathrooms. A formal dining room, sitting room, study, nook, library and two other 'lounging spaces'—she didn't even know what to call them. A large pantry filled with stacks and stacks of tinned food, spices and bakery ingredients.

The modern kitchen gleamed, full of state-of-the-art appliances, with a few instructions in a folder at the side. In the middle of the kitchen table was a huge basket, packed with groceries and some fun snacks. The fridge had all the essentials for breakfast, lunch and dinner. She followed the instructions and flicked the switch on the coffee machine as she prepared some eggs on the stove of the range cooker.

This place was really out of this world. She could swear she was in a Bond movie. Any minute now some super-villain would walk through one of the doors and ask what she was doing in their house. She glanced at the clock on the wall. It was after seven. The slopes here were already open.

She picked up the phone and dialled the number connecting her to the resort to arrange a pickup at the chalet. The owner really had thought of everything.

Running upstairs, she pulled on her ski gear, goggles and gloves. Her ski equipment had been left at the front door last night, so she was good to go.

She moved through to the main room and stopped. A Christmas tree. She hadn't even thought about that.

She smiled and moved over, touching the beautiful, colour-coordinated decorations. Of course, these would have been done by a professional decorator. Not the normal hotchpotch that she put out year after year, which had started to look bedraggled. A large glistening star crowned the tree and Paige looked around, wondering if she was actually still sleeping in the bed upstairs. This was too good. Too perfect.

She sank down into the large red sofa for a moment, overwhelmed by it all.

It all seemed too much. Too much for one person. Too much for one little doctor who was here on her own. Too much for someone who should probably just have given themselves a shake and gone back to work, instead of agreeing to take some time off. When Leo had told her this place was used for respite, had he known that she was contemplating whether she still wanted to be a doctor? Or maybe the Baron only wanted health professionals in his resorts—would he be angry if it turned out Paige didn't want to be one any more? Had Leo known how spectacular this place would be when he'd sent her here?

Somehow, she thought that he might.

The thoughts just kept swirling round and round in her head.

She breathed for a few moments, trying to get some perspective. Telling herself that the local police were not about to show up here, demand to see her papers, and accuse her of breaking and entering. The code that she'd been sent had opened the door, and turned off the alarm with no problem at all.

This was definitely where she was supposed to be.

There was a large fireplace in front of her. This spot would be a spectacular place to snuggle tonight. She could eat some of the chocolate in the giant basket and find a book in the library she had yet to properly explore. It didn't matter that she'd brought several of her own—exploring someone else's library would be fun. This really was her idea of heaven.

She wandered back to the main door. There was a smiley face on the store cupboard at the entrance and she pulled it open curiously, then stopped dead.

It wasn't really a 'store' cupboard. It was a full ski equipment closet. She could see boots, poles, skis, clothing, goggles and other equipment lining the walls and methodically stored. As she wandered along the walls her hands reached out to touch some of the items. She'd brought her own ski equipment, but instantly recognised that this was prestige equipment. Items she'd never be able to purchase in a million years.

She moved back and looked at the list on the wall, naming everything in the store cupboard. If she had the time, she could cost up the entire contents and likely weep.

The list also had instructions, stating that all equipment was free to use, a request to keep the store tidy, to follow guidelines for care of equipment—there was a shelf with a variety of products, including boot-liners and ski wax.

Paige walked back down the rack of skis, her hand automatically lifting to touch some. There was a distinctive gold logo that she recognised. The phrase *Fastest skis on the planet* was the tagline of the exclusive brand. She ran her fingers down the top of the ski, her mouth slightly dry. She'd probably never get a chance to try this brand of ski again. There were six pairs in a row, all of varying length, some on-piste, some all-mountain. Of course, there was a pair just her size.

There was a buzz at the front door. It must be the driver from the resort. She didn't let herself think too much, just lifted the skis carefully, along with a set of matching poles, and made her way to the door.

The driver gave her a cheerful nod. He lifted his hands. 'Bad weather expected,' he said. 'Best get in as much skiing as possible.'

Paige was surprised but, then again, she hadn't even looked at any weather reports. 'Today?'

He shrugged. 'Definitely tomorrow and a

few days after. High winds and storms expected.' He lifted her equipment and carried it to the vehicle. 'They didn't mention today, but look at those dark clouds.' He pointed to a dark smudge in the distance. 'At this time in the morning? I think the weather might be coming in early.'

Paige frowned but then looked back towards her chalet. 'If I have to stay inside for a few days, it won't be a problem.'

'You have food? Wine? You might want to get some supplies before you head back here.'

She climbed into the front seat of the vehicle next to him. 'I might grab a few things. But the chalet came fully prepared. I think I'll be okay.' She leaned forward as he started the engine. 'Tell me about the slopes. What's your recommendation?'

The driver began talking and Paige settled back into the comfortable seat to listen. Even if she only had one day to ski to begin with, it would still be a good start.

She watched as they started down the twisting road, her mind flashing back to last night and the grumpy handsome man. She was a little fascinated about the hospital being renovated up the road from the chalet. Maybe, if she got a chance, she could take a walk up and have a look around. If it had been used in the First World War she could only imagine the history of the place.

She was trying to pretend she wasn't a little curious about the guy too. Why had he been up at the hospital at night? Did he work there? Was he a businessman? The suit had been a bit flash. An accountant maybe, or someone overseeing the work? If a hospital was being renovated, shouldn't it have been tradesmen and contractors that she'd come across, instead of a man in a suit?

Paige leaned back and looked out of the window at the winter landscape. She could think about the mystery of the hospital, and the man, later. Right now, there were slopes to explore.

He loved it. The sensation of moving at speed, making tiny adjustments with his weight and the curve of his body, all to enhance the smoothness of his run. He could do this in his sleep. Skiing had been part of his life since he was a child. For Stefan, skiing was as easy as breathing.

He'd been on the slopes since first light. It was starting to get busier now, and that always slightly annoyed him. He'd skied on some of the most difficult runs on the planet: Harakiri in Austria, Corbet's Couloir in Wyoming, La Grave in France, and Delirium Dive in Alberta. There were, of course, equally challenging black runs at the many resorts in Switzerland but, unfortunately, today's weather meant that all black runs in the local vicinity were closed. Stefan had to content himself with an easier red run, and it was busier than it should be.

He expertly glided around someone stuck midway down the run. Another skier who'd moved up from the beginner slopes before they were really ready to. It was common here, which was why Stefan usually stuck to the black runs. Of course, they too had their fair share of skiers who tried them before they were ready; however, the traffic was always a bit less frantic on the tougher runs.

He'd stayed out longer than he'd intended to. Serious skiers, like himself, were usually first on the slopes and finished while most of those at the resort were still eating breakfast. The late starters had now all caught up with him and the slopes seemed cluttered, and just waiting for accidental collisions. There was a weather warning for the next few days, extremely high winds and general storms. It was unlikely most of the people here would be able to ski then, so, like them, he was trying to get as much time in as possible.

Part of his early morning run today had been about shaking off his frustration at the delays in the project. His frustrations had boiled over last night too, when what seemed like another tourist had been driving on the twisty and precarious mountain road without enough due care and attention. It had turned out to be one of the private drivers from the nearby airport—but that still didn't excuse the fact he'd come around the corner with half his vehicle on the wrong side of the road.

It hadn't helped that his very feisty passenger had called Stefan out on his behaviour almost immediately. He couldn't get that accent out of his head. He'd worked with doctors from all over the world, but the Scottish accent was entirely unique, and sometimes almost impossible to understand. Whoever she was, she'd been headed for the billionaire chalet just down from the hospital. He'd never had time to find out who owned it—maybe it was her?—but, whoever she was, she had a fiery glint in her eye, and a take-no-prisoners attitude.

He'd liked it. Pity he hadn't taken the time to find out her name. But last night his temper had been shot, and his mood irritable. When he'd finally got to bed, his mind had been fixated on the brown-haired, dark-eyed woman who'd put him firmly in his place.

A flash of red crossed his vision and he momentarily slowed, before realising the skier had passed him as if he were barely moving. Something twisted in his guts. Whoever this skier was, they were skilled, and fast—very, very fast.

There was a well-known signature gold flash from the back of the skis they were using and he groaned. Ten-thousand-dollar skis. Of course.

He lowered his body, moving closer to the white packed snow beneath him as he curved into the slope, picking up speed along the way. He didn't want to catch the other skier. That would be juvenile. But he didn't want to be passed as if he were an absolute beginner, or the oldest man on the slope.

Wind whistled past him, hitting his cheeks in a satisfying surge. His tinted ski goggles kept his eyes protected and his vision clear as he continued down the slope, gaining speed all the way.

He pretended he wasn't fixated on the figure in red. It was a woman. He could tell that now from the curves. She was starting to slow down, clearly getting ready for the end of the run. But Stefan had never been the guy to slow down. Adrenaline made him remain low and still hugging the slope as he neared her.

He passed others on the way down, all slowing, but Stefan waited until the end before pulling up sharply, turning sideways and sending a huge spray of snow into the sky above.

Several people behind the barrier at the bottom were showered lightly with snow. A few glared as they wiped their sleeves. He turned his head from side to side, but the skier in red had already disappeared.

He shook his head. It was too busy now, and his concentration was going. There was a thud behind him as someone misjudged their speed and crashed into the safety barrier. Stefan clicked off his skis and stepped over to pick up the crumpled heap of a teenage boy. 'Okay?' he checked.

The boy pulled his helmet off and groaned, rubbing one of his legs as his two friends glided to a more elegant halt next to them. Stefan bent a bit lower to check the boy's face. 'Really, are you okay? Can you stand?'

The boy put his weight on his legs and grimaced. 'Sorry, I thought I could stop in time.'

He looked completely embarrassed, and his friends weren't helping as they started to barrage him with good-humoured abuse. Stefan appreciated it. He'd been this teenager once.

'You live and learn,' he said simply. 'You'll be covered in bruises tomorrow though.'

The boy nodded and Stefan left him with his friends, picking up his skis and heading towards the two coffee shops. One was flash and fashionable, with light colours and floor-to-ceiling windows after being refurbished in the last few years, but Stefan headed into the other. Filled with wood and with smaller windows, this place was a mixture of café and bar. All orders were taken at the broad wooden bar, with customers expected to collect their drinks and food when they were ready. There were two traditional fireplaces, one at either end of the brick building, both surrounded by an array of worn armchairs and sofas, all in a variety of colours. Stefan's favourite was probably the most worn in the entire café. It was dark grey, some kind of velour that had patches on the arms and the imprint of probably twenty years' worth of skiers' behinds.

He moved to the bar and ordered a hot chocolate—a drink that just didn't work well in the Hollywood Hills, but as soon as he reached here it was the first thing he ordered.

For breakfast, he ordered a large bowl of muesli. Through the small windows he could see dark clouds rolling in from the west. If he ate now, he'd be able to concentrate when he got back up the mountain to see if the contractors were all on site. It was essential he ensured the work moved along on time.

As he waited for his order, he could hear chatter and laughter from the other skiers. There was what looked like a school party gathered near the entrance. Some families, lots of couples and groups of friends. The chair lift constantly hummed with figures with their dangling skis on their feet methodically ascending the mountain. The parallel ski lift had the odd mishap, resulting in someone landing on their back and a single rogue ski generally disappearing in inevitably the wrong direction.

Stefan smiled as he lifted his hot chocolate topped with cream and bowl of muesli, making his way in pure habit to the large grey chair with its back to him. As he moved sideways to sit down, he noticed the figure in his chair, a red ski jacket lying on the nearby sofa. Because he hadn't realised anyone was sitting there, he was far too close and his leg bumped an elbow, sending coffee sloshing to the floor.

He spoke instantly in German, apologising profusely. His eyes caught the stack of toast on the table in front of the armchair, butter and jam next to it. He realised his second mistake. This person had to be from the UK. He switched language. 'I'm so sorry. I didn't realise someone was sitting here.'

Dark eyes looked up at him, scanning his ski gear. There was a real flare of annoyance, and then her forehead creased and her gaze narrowed.

'You,' she said accusingly.

It took him a few seconds. Red ski gear. He looked sideways to where all the skis were currently stowed for the patrons of the café. Sure enough, the gold-logoed designer skis caught his eye.

'Do you always ski like some flash idiot?' the female voice continued.

The thick Scottish accent slayed him as

pieces started to drop in place. The woman from last night.

'Do you always hire a driver that drives like an idiot?'

Her mouth fell open and her mug tipped to the side again, sloshing more coffee. He caught it and wrapped his hand around it. 'Apologies, let me get you another.' He gave a quick order to the woman behind the bar and slid the red jacket along the sofa, sitting down in its place.

The woman looked at him again. 'Do you just steamroller yourself through life?'

He smiled. Spark. And sass. Relief washed over him. After he'd finished his training as a doctor, he'd completed two six-month placements in the UK, one in London, one in Edinburgh. He'd loved the people, their straight talking and no messing around. He actually missed it. Surgery in the Hollywood Hills with a prestigious client group was a very different ballgame.

He leaned over and held out his hand. 'Stefan Bachmann.'

She eyed his hand as if it were growing microscopic bugs, before wiping her own palm on her red salopettes and shaking it firmly. 'Paige McLeod.'

'Where are you from in Scotland, Paige?'

'Oh, no.' She wagged a finger at him. 'You don't get to sit down all smug after, one…' she counted off on her fingers '…you tried to blame us for a near miss last night. Two, you tried to drown me in snow with your flashy and, may I add…' she leaned forward '…unsafe stop earlier. And three, you just bulldozered past me and spilled my coffee.' She pointed to the table in front of her. 'If you'd knocked my toast, it would have been game over.'

He laughed. 'Don't get between a Scots girl and her breakfast. Is there anything you don't want to blame me for?'

She looked at her half-filled coffee cup. 'Nope, I think everything is absolutely your fault.' Her dark eyes flashed and it was the first time he really got a chance to look at her properly. Last night had been too dark. Even now, the light from outside wasn't particularly good and the lighting in the café was deliberately dull. But that couldn't hide how attractive this Scottish woman was. Her long, dark brown hair was pulled back in a ponytail. Her pale skin was clear, but revealed fine bones and dark brown eyes that had a lot of fire in them. There was no obvious surgery. Who was this woman? She was skiing with very expensive equipment.

She was staying in one of the finest properties on the mountainside, one that no one really knew anything about. Was she the billionaire, or was her husband? His eyes took a fleeting glance at her hand. No ring. He was surprised by the fact he liked that. She moved her head slightly and something twisted in him. Was that a faint bruise on her cheek?

The waiter behind the bar gave him a wave and Stefan stood up to collect the fresh coffee, setting it down next to Paige's toast. 'Coffee can be replaced. Here you go. Anyhow, it's partly your fault. You are, after all, sitting in my seat.'

She'd started buttering her toast and looked up incredulously. '*Your* seat?' He could tell she was enjoying this sparring.

He lifted his bowl of muesli and shrugged. 'It's my favourite. Whenever I come here, it's where I like to sit.'

'So, you think you own everything?'

He shook his head. 'No. But don't you have a favourite chair in a favourite café back home?'

She thought for a moment and nodded. 'Actually, I do. There's a café with old-fashioned bench seats opposite where I work. They have a special of the day, apple or blackberry tarts, custard doughnuts, caramel cakes, Victoria sponge or homemade Swiss roll. I make it my business to make sure the special is up to standard.'

It was a longer answer than he'd expected. She clearly did have a favourite café.

'So then, we're not so different.' There was a hint of satisfaction in his voice.

But it was clear she was not letting him get away with that. 'Don't bet on it.' She arched her eyebrows and then changed the subject. 'You're local?'

'Yes, and no.'

She opened the jam. 'Are we talking in riddles now?'

Stefan wrinkled his nose. 'My family are from around here. I grew up here, but I've worked away for most of my adult life. I come back at least three times a year, and I hope to be back a bit more.'

Paige looked at him with interest. 'Because of the hospital.'

He nodded. 'Because of the hospital.'

She took a bite of her toast and closed her eyes. 'Bliss,' she sighed, then took another bite.

After a few seconds, she brought her attention back to him. 'So, what do you do? Do you own the place—the hospital?'

'Yes, and no.' Then he laughed, realising what he'd done.

She leaned back in his chair. 'Let me just get comfortable in *your* chair. Because it's clear you're going to talk in riddles all day.' There was something about the grin on her face as she said it. He liked the fact that Scottish Paige had kept him on his toes from the moment she'd met him.

Paige turned her head to the window momentarily. In the last ten minutes snow had started pelting the windows outside and a dark cloud had moved over the area, causing the inside of the café to look quite gloomy. There were a number of people leaving the slopes now and heading back down to the town beneath.

'Looks like we came in at the right time. My driver this morning warned me to go and pick up some provisions down in the main resort as the weather forecast wasn't good. I don't think I'll bother now. The chalet has more than enough food for the next few days.'

'You're staying alone?'

She blinked and looked straight at him. It was a straightforward question, but she immediately wondered why he'd asked.

She gave a nod. 'Yes, there's plenty of room for more people. But it's just me. As far as I know, there won't be anyone joining me.'

She could almost hear her friend from work screaming in her ear. Red flag. Why would you tell a stranger that? You've told him you're alone, in a remote chalet, in a strange country. But, although she'd just met Stefan, she didn't feel wary of him. She wasn't at all worried about him knowing she was alone in the chalet. In fact, it was probably good that someone who was working further up the mountainside knew she was alone, just in case she needed help with anything.

What would she do in a power cut? If the pipes froze? She didn't know the answer to any of these questions, although she had a sneaking suspicion the answers might actually be in one of the very organised folders in the chalet. But it would be nice to have a backup plan.

A few other skiers were standing at one of the small windows, glancing up the slopes and having a worried-looking conversation. It made her a little uncomfortable, so she turned her attention back to Stefan, who was finishing his muesli. 'Hey, you didn't finish your riddle.'

He set his bowl down and then held up both hands. 'Yeah, the hospital was bought by the company I work for, but I'm also a shareholder. They were looking for a property in the Alps and obviously I knew of the place because I'd been brought up here. The company bought the old hospital with the purpose of refurbishing it into a new respite facility.'

'So, who needs a very expensive respite facility in the Alps these days?'

He gave her a careful look and she realised the words might have sounded judgemental—the last thing she was.

'The main people using this facility will be those requiring, or requesting, some kind of surgery, and those who need to undergo treatment of some kind and don't want to do it in the public domain. But not everyone coming to the clinic will be a private patient.'

She frowned. 'Who else will be coming?' Her head was already full of international models, actors and pop stars. Maybe even a few politicians.

There was a strange noise. A kind of shift.

'I work for another organisation...' Stefan's eyes widened and he stopped mid-sentence.

Then she could swear the ground moved beneath her feet.

'Everyone get down!' yelled Stefan. 'Avalanche!'

Paige did the opposite. She stood up. There were people outside. Lots of them. Next minute there was an arm around her middle, pulling her down and behind one of the sofas.

The noise was simultaneously increasing in volume to a loud roar. Everything around her was shaking. Plates and glasses were crashing to the ground. She was conscious of the full length of Stefan's body tucked behind hers. He had one hand still around her waist, and the other over the top of her head.

The noise was so loud now, people were screaming and then there was an almighty crash and everything went dark.

Paige was frozen. A punch. A ricochet off her head. Pain in her shoulder and side. She was having flashbacks to her attacks in the hospital.

She pulled her hands over her head and curled inwards, trying to stave off the panic that was threatening to take over her body. Her heart thudded in her chest as a quiet voice said in her ear, 'Paige, just breathe.' It was calm. It was steady. And warm breath hit the skin at the side of her neck. She was lying in an almost intimate position with a perfect stranger, who could clearly feel her starting to panic.

Someone was crying and the sound seemed to flick some kind of switch inside her. Paige took a deep breath and sat up, pushing her hair out of her eyes and taking in the chaotic scene around her. Most people were on the ground, a few were clutching arms or faces. Broken dishes were strewn across the floor. The lights flickered.

She felt a movement behind her. A hand on her forearm. 'Okay?'

She nodded, realising that Stefan had moved. In a dazed silence she watched as he moved across the room, going from person to person. It took her only a few seconds to realise what he was doing.

She stood up, steadying herself on the grey armchair, which was still upright. She moved over next to Stefan, where he was wrapping something around a woman's arm. 'You're a doctor?'

He looked up, obviously surprised to see her on her feet. 'A surgeon,' he said quietly as he tied off the makeshift bandage.

Of course. He wasn't some kind of businessman involved in a hospital. He was a doctor—probably what a lot of people needed right now.

'What can I do?' she asked.

His gaze narrowed. 'Do you have any training?'

'I'm a doctor,' she replied. 'I work in A&E.'

Surprise flashed across his eyes and he nodded in the other direction. 'Take a look at the people on the other side of the room. Check for anything major. We can leave the minor stuff for now. We need to get outside.'

Paige swallowed. Outside. Oh, no. She grabbed her red jacket and stuffed it under her arm, following his instructions to do a quick check on the people across the room. There were lots of dazed and scraped people there. But there were no major head injuries, no obvious broken limbs. Most people just needed to be picked up, assisted into a chair and told to take a breath.

Within a few minutes she was back, red jacket on, and standing next to the doorway, waiting for Stefan. His black ski gear now seemed ominous, but she tried to push those thoughts out of her head.

'Stay next to me,' he instructed, 'until we assess the situation.'

The door opened with a few hard pushes. Everything was white.

But not quite. There were trees, branches and bushes. Pieces of twisted metal—probably the chair lift—poked in awkward angles out of the snow.

'Oh, no,' Stefan said quietly, and Paige turned quickly to look in the same direction as him.

'What?' she said automatically.

And then she saw it.

The avalanche had swept down the mountainside, mainly to their right. But the road that led down the mountain, and back to the civilisation, was completely blocked. They, and all the potentially injured people around them, were trapped.

CHAPTER THREE

STEFAN BLINKED. A COMPLETE DISASTER. He couldn't remember the last time there had been an avalanche in this part of the Alps. But nowhere was ever completely safe. Where there was snow, there was a risk of avalanche.

He didn't even want to think about how long the road would take to clear. All he could see was mounds of rubble underneath the snow. He started praying there weren't people in there.

A shout caught his attention, and he realised one of the staff from the resort was shouting instructions. He turned to Paige. A doctor. When she'd told him, for a moment he'd been surprised. He'd been fairly certain that in the few seconds of the avalanche she'd seemed as if she was having a panic attack. He really wanted to know more, but now just wasn't the time.

'Can you assist?' he asked.

She nodded without hesitation. He reached over and grabbed her arm. 'Then come with me.'

When it came to an avalanche, the usual rules went out of the window. You didn't take time to assess. You didn't think about all the risks. You didn't wait for help. You immediately tried to rescue those around you.

He strode towards the man who was shouting—a large man, dressed in dark snow gear with yellow flashes and a bright hat on his head. Stefan didn't waste any time. 'Stefan and Paige, both doctors. Where do you need us?'

The man replied rapidly in German. Stefan could see the confusion on Paige's face, so listened carefully, gave the man some more information, then nodded in agreement. He turned to Paige.

'Franco, works here, he's a ski guide, but is also part of the mountain rescue scheme. He's going to organise teams to identify anyone injured or stuck. We've to set up a base back in the café, and they'll bring them all to us.'

'Shouldn't we dig too? Isn't it more important to get those who are trapped out?'

Stefan hesitated. He didn't really want to stand around right now. There were a few injuries already in the café. But none seemed imminently dangerous. People could suffocate in the snow. If they needed to dig first and provide medical aid later, that was fine with him.

Hysterical voices and shouts were everywhere. This was a chaotic scene, and they needed to be systematic here.

He spoke again to Franco, who at first shook his head and then sighed. He finally nodded, then directed them to where another man had appeared with some shovels and probes. Franco directed small teams of willing volunteers to different parts of the piled snow, with another man bringing out some equipment from the dismantled hut at the bottom of the chair lift.

'What's that?' asked Paige.

'I assume it's a radio receiver for any emergency locator beacons.' He looked at her, wondering how experienced she was at skiing. She'd certainly come down that slope like a pro, so he was assuming she had some knowledge. 'You do carry an avalanche transceiver?'

He could see recognition on her face. 'Of

course.' She tapped her shoulder. 'It came with the jacket, sewed into the lining.'

He nodded. 'I'm hoping everyone who was skiing today had one in place. It might be the only way we can find them. Time isn't on our side.' Something dark crossed his face.

Stefan grabbed two shovels and turned to Paige. 'We go to the patch we're allocated and dig where we find any sign there might be someone underneath. In the meantime, the experts will search for signals. They'll redirect the teams if they pick up a signal.'

Franco turned to face the mountain, lifted his hand and drew invisible lines in the air, mapping out eight large squares. There was no time for anything else and they all knew it.

Stefan turned to a few other adults who were standing, shocked, near the café. 'Can you help? Can you dig?'

His voice seemed to jerk them out of their shock. One woman appeared, with tears streaming down her face. 'Yes,' she said, nodding. Another few people seemed to realise that Franco was trying to organise a rescue and came to help.

Paige looked pale. She was already fair-skinned, but now appeared a little sickly. Stefan touched her shoulder. 'Can you do this?' She might be a doctor but Paige, like everyone else here, could be injured. Maybe he hadn't been able to protect her in the café the way he'd wanted to. Or was he pushing when he shouldn't?

She tugged her bright hat a little further over her ears. 'Absolutely. Let's go.'

It was clear that many people were still dazed, some searching for friends or family with no idea where they might be. Stefan's instinct was to run over and try to help everyone. He saw Paige glancing in one direction, with the same thought practically written on her face.

He put his hand on hers. 'I know,' he said in a low voice. 'I know. I want to run over to them all. But we have to be methodical about this. And we're time-limited here.' He hated saying that out loud. But people buried under snow could suffocate. They were absolutely time-limited here. Digging people out as quickly as possible was essential. 'We have to stick to the patch we're allocated. Franco seems the most experienced here. Let's see if we can help.' He looked further up the mountain. 'We have to remember this could happen again.'

Paige gave a visible shudder but lifted her shovel and followed him. Two other people joined them. The snow in their area was littered with debris. It was hard to determine what everything was. He extended his probe. The collapsible fibreglass pole was like a tent rod and could be used to determine the location and depth of snow where a person could be buried. Stefan dropped to his knees, tugging at anything sticking up in the snow. There were a variety of shouts. The man next to him tugged at part of a ski. It was still attached to a leg. The four of them dug frantically to reveal a shocked woman, who coughed madly as soon as they pulled the snow from around her face.

Stefan gave a few instructions to one of the men, then looked at the other three. 'Time matters. We can dig her out completely in a few minutes. Let's check if we can find anyone else.'

Another dark blotch was the elbow of a man's jacket. It only took a few moments to free his face from snow and let him take a few breaths. The second man stayed with him as Stefan and Paige moved on.

Franco gave a shout. He came running over. 'Signal in your area.' He turned his receiver and pointed at one specific point. 'There!'

He used the probe a few times, until finally he got a hit. It could be anything—part of a tree or rock, but, with the assistance of a beacon, he hoped it was a person. Stefan started shovelling straight away. Digging frantically was difficult, and he had to still all his senses. The last thing he wanted to do was cause someone more harm by shovelling too near their face.

Within seconds he saw a flash of pink. 'We've got something.'

His stomach lurched as he and Paige dropped to their knees again and started to pull snow away with their hands. The flash of pink enlarged, and Stefan quickly realised by the size of the limb that this was a child.

Franco met his gaze. 'You got this?'

Stefan knew that he must have picked up another signal. 'Absolutely,' he replied. 'Go.'

Paige was shaking. Her hands moved rapidly, throwing snow away from the pink ski suit as they tried to determine which way was up for the little person underneath them. 'Foot!' she yelled and moved instantly, elbowing Stefan to push him further along so they could scoop out the snow nearer where this child's head would be. The little leg hadn't moved yet.

Stefan was trying not to think about the time. Was it more than five minutes? If an experienced skier had been caught in the avalanche they might have had an instinct to create some space around their head. Some might even have an avalanche airbag haversack—a device that would inflate and bring them to the surface of the snow during the actual avalanche. Some parent, somewhere, had clearly had the sense to put an avalanche transmitter on their child. He only hoped they would find the parent too as he continued to dig.

Curly blonde hair appeared under his hands. Paige let out a gasp and immediately helped move the packed snow. The girl looked around seven or eight, her face exposed and skin cold. Stefan moved forward, his face right next to the little girl's. He was hoping and praying she was in shock right now. He breathed on her face, talking quietly, then tried to position himself to give her some rescue breaths.

'Let me,' said Paige. She knew exactly what he was trying to do. But she was slimmer and lighter and slipped her head into the tight space next to the child. He couldn't see properly but, after a few moments, there was a sound from the child. A splutter, followed by a loud howl.

Stefan had his head down next to Paige

and the child. His eyes caught sight of something else. He touched Paige. 'I think I have someone else—can I leave you?'

She nodded and he moved quickly, grabbing his shovel and probe again. Was he imagining something or were those fingertips?

Darn it. He would have missed them. Experienced skiers knew to try and create a space around their face, to put one arm upward in the hope of being seen, and even to mimic backward swimming during an avalanche. Stefan had read all the stories, heard all the advice, but he'd never experienced anything like this before.

Sure enough, fingertips were just barely protruding through the snow. He shovelled quickly, shouting over to the rescuer who was next to the woman they'd first found to give him some help. This man was clearly deeper than any of the other people they had found.

Sweat was pouring off Stefan. He still hadn't done a time check. He knew that the best chance of survival for anyone caught in an avalanche was for them to be found in the first fifteen minutes. Chances of survival decreased sharply after that. They must rapidly be approaching that now. He could also remember that somewhere, deep at the back of his mind, he'd read something about the best way to dig people out. Stefan was cursing that he couldn't recall the details. He kept going, even though the muscles in his arms were burning. He didn't even know the name of the guy digging next to him, he just knew that this stranger was working every bit as hard as he was.

There was a high-pitched wail and it cut right through him. He looked up, just in time to see a woman drop on her knees next to Paige. She started helping to dig the little girl out. It must be the mother. He was relieved. He'd half-expected her to be buried in the snow too.

The wind was picking up, making it difficult to anchor himself in place. It also resulted in the light, more powdery snow swirling around him like a smokescreen. He kept digging, finally seeing some dark hair and moving quickly to delicately scoop the snow out from around his face. The man made a huge splutter, coughing and choking, and almost immediately Stefan could hear the wheeze in his breathing. He would bet this man had broken some ribs.

A few other people came to join them.

'What's your name?' asked Stefan, first in German, then in French.

'Rafe,' came the spluttered reply.

'I'm Stefan. I'm a surgeon. I'll take a proper look at you when we get you out of here. I think it's going to take a little time.'

The man gave a nod but didn't reply. At least he was conscious. Franco tapped Stefan on the shoulder. 'Let these other folks do the digging for a moment, Doc,' he said. 'I need you and the other doc inside, assessing the patients.'

Stefan straightened up. It was difficult to see around him right now. The wind and swirling snow meant he could only see a few feet away. Paige was closest to him and he could see her assisting lifting the blonde-haired little girl from the snow. The mother was understandably hysterical, but also getting in the way.

He couldn't see properly, and he certainly couldn't hear but, from the actions, he could tell Paige was talking to the mother, trying to placate and calm her down in order to look after her daughter. Within a few seconds, it was clear she'd had some impact. The mother stepped back a little, allowing Paige to bend over the little girl and do something else. She'd told him she worked in A&E. Paige clearly had experience dealing with upset and anxious relatives.

He nodded at Franco and stepped back himself to allow the other men to take over. He gave a few instructions about taking care around the man's chest and torso and followed Franco back to the entrance of the café.

The café on the other side thankfully had its floor-to-ceiling windows intact. Whilst Stefan might have never known of an avalanche in these parts, the planners had clearly taken no chances and he imagined the windows had specially toughened glass. It was a blessing.

'We've taken everyone with injuries in here. Another few people have come forward who can help, two who are nurses and one who is a physio.'

Stefan nodded. 'Are there any supplies?'

'We have a medical station with a bit more than is usual in a first aid kit. Some splints, and inflatables for fractures. A few stitching kits.'

Stefan nodded. Fractures and wounds requiring a few stitches were probably the most serious injuries usually dealt with here.

'I may have to go up to the hospital,' he

said. 'I have more equipment there, and that part of the road looks as if it's not blocked.'

Franco pointed to the road horizontal to the resorts, café and lifts. 'The avalanche seemed to come down almost diagonally. Look at the amount of snow. It will take days for them to clear the road and get us out of here.'

Stefan looked up. His skin prickled as he realised just how serious their situation was. Paige appeared at his shoulder as Franco started to speak again. 'And, with these high winds, it's unlikely we'll be able to get any helicopter assistance.'

His mind was working overtime now. He'd have to come up with some kind of plan. He nodded to Paige. 'Let us see how everyone is doing and then make a decision about what comes next. Do you think there is anyone else buried in the snow?'

Franco's expression was deadly serious. 'It's impossible to know. We're trying to do an account of everyone, to establish if anyone is missing from any party. But if there were any solo skiers, then unless I find a beacon signal we'll just never know.' He laid his gloved hand on Stefan's arm. 'Leave that part to me. We can chat later.'

'What's happening?' asked Paige, 'I got pulled away before I was finished.'

Stefan nodded and led her inside the café. Three other people were standing near the doorway, waiting for them. 'Are you the other medical personnel that can assist?'

They nodded.

'I'm Stefan, I'm local and a surgeon. This is Paige, a doctor from the UK who works in A&E.'

A woman with fair hair spoke next. 'I'm Lynn, a nurse from England. I work in orthopaedics, and this is Joe, my partner, who works in Theatre.' Joe was already stripping off his jacket and hat, getting prepared to work.

The third person spoke up too. 'Cathy, I'm a cardiac physio, but just ask me to do what you need. I'll tell you if I need instruction.'

Paige stepped forward. 'Let's do this as a triage system like we use in A&E. Anyone who is okay, or has minor injuries and can wait, can go into the café next door right now. Any head injury, abdomen injury, possible break or wound that needs cleaning and stitching stays here.'

Stefan watched with interest. Paige had pulled off her red jacket again and tugged her dark hair from her knitted hat. Her ski goggles seemed to have disappeared. She turned to Stefan. 'Will we be able to get to the hospital if required?'

He nodded. 'I think so. I also have a vehicle up there. Once we've treated everyone, I can hike up and bring my car down to transport anyone up. From what Franco and I could see, that part of the road above looks clear.'

Paige nodded thoughtfully. 'My chalet is probably accessible too. If people need somewhere to sleep it might be useful. And there's lots of food too.'

Stefan lifted his hand, hating to say these words. 'A bit of caution. The hospital is only halfway renovated.'

'What does that mean?' asked Joe quickly.

'There's water and electricity. Several rooms and staff areas are ready. There are functional operating theatres and a number of stock and equipment should have been delivered today before the road was blocked.'

'What kind?' Joe was clearly thinking ahead.

'The furnishings were already in place, but some surgical equipment, medical supplies, pharmacy goods and sundries were all arriving early this morning. The hospital was supposed to open soon, and these deliveries had never been cancelled.'

'Lucky,' breathed Paige.

'Only lucky if they arrived,' said Lynn.

'Let's get started,' said Stefan, praying that by the time he got up to the hospital he wouldn't find the place empty.

They moved quickly, assessing all the people. 'We've been lucky,' murmured Paige. 'Someone told me this place is usually much busier, but it looks like a number had already left because of the weather warning for later today.'

'Thank goodness,' agreed Stefan. 'I bet some of these people wish they'd left earlier today too.'

'Don't you?'

He looked at her and shook his head. 'No,' he said honestly. 'I'm glad I'm here. I'll do what I can to help.'

She pressed her lips together and he thought he glimpsed a sheen of tears in her eyes. But Paige was determined. She'd pulled her long hair back in a ponytail and pushed the sleeves up on her thermal underclothes. She'd removed her ski boots and was moving around in thick socks. As they continued to work, they moved away from each other.

Every few minutes the main door would open and Franco or some of his team would appear, carrying someone who'd been dug out of the snow on a portable stretcher. Thank goodness the resort had equipment around.

When they'd assessed everyone in the room, Stefan met with Paige and the others. 'What do you have?'

Paige looked worried. 'A seven-year-old female with a fractured tib and fib, a forty-year-old male with a suspected head injury that we need to observe, a thirty-eight-year-old woman with suspected rib fractures and a definite ulna and radius fracture.'

Stefan nodded. 'I've Rafe, the man who's just been dug out. His temperature is borderline hypothermic, breathing erratic. He has rib fractures too. I've two other females with suspected ankle fractures.'

Lynn, Joe and Cathy listed their patients, the majority requiring stitches, one woman in the early stage of pregnancy with cramping but no bleeding, an older man with known angina who'd lost his meds, and a diabetic whose insulin pen had shattered.

Franco appeared next to them, the door banging loudly behind him and the high wind whistling in. 'What's the verdict?' He had a satellite phone in his hand.

'I've got nine people I should take up to the hospital if I can. And a whole host of others we need to clean up and stitch.'

Franco nodded and handed him the phone. 'We have three satellite phones, so this one is for you. The cafés have plenty of food and are comfortable enough. Those who are well enough can stay here with myself and the rest of the staff.'

'How long until help arrives?' asked Lynn.

Franco and Stefan exchanged glances, which Paige didn't miss. 'What does that mean?' He could hear the tension in her voice.

He turned to face her. 'The road block is extensive. I have no idea how long it will take for them to move the snow and rubble so there is access again.'

'Surely there's another way to get people out?' People. Not her, he noted. She wasn't worrying about herself, she was worrying about their new patients, and potentially the rest of the people who could be stranded here.

Franco's deep voice interrupted his thoughts. 'In normal circumstances the emergency services and mountain rescue would be able to bring helicopters to get people in, and out. But…' he gestured towards the sky '…no one can fly in those winds. Too dangerous. We probably don't even want anyone outside.'

Realisation dawned on Paige's face. 'So we're stuck here?'

'For now,' replied Stefan. 'I'm sure we can manage.' He was saying the words without really knowing if they were true. He could only hope the supplies that were ordered for the hospital had actually arrived.

'I'll be able to do some X-rays, put the plaster casts on, even set some bones if required.'

Stefan nodded. He was actually glad she was here. Most docs who worked in A&E had some experience of plaster casting—particularly any who'd covered a Saturday night shift and had to patch up those after a drunken night out. There wasn't so much of that in Hollywood. He'd put plaster casts on arms and legs after cosmetic surgery procedures, but they were few and far between.

Paige gave him a wary look. 'So, what you're basically saying is we're trapped here, with all these people, and the hopeful medical supplies left in a half-finished hospital, for an unknown amount of time.'

The thing he'd first noticed about her and admired—the way she was blunt and to the point. All eyes were on him and Franco gave him a half-smile. For the next few days these were his staff, and it was up to him to deal with them.

'When you put it like that, yes, we're stuck here and have patients to deal with. I'm sure we'll all be fine.'

Paige's gaze met his and she straightened her shoulders. 'In that case, let's finish our stitching, check all wounds are sound and not leave anyone behind we think might deteriorate in any way. It will be difficult enough to get everyone up to the hospital safely. We don't want to make unnecessary trips.' She sighed, put her hands on her hips and arched her back. 'Is there a kitchen?'

He nodded.

'Okay, on the last journey back up, we'll stop at the chalet and collect all the food and take it up with us.' She nodded at Cathy and Lynn. 'I also have some clothes there that we can share out.'

It was as if someone had flicked a switch in her. He'd seen it a few times now. Once, just after the avalanche had hit. Then again for a few seconds, when she'd been asked to help. On both occasions it was as if Paige went on automatic pilot and started performing as a doctor. And it wasn't just that. She was good. From what he'd observed, her decisions seemed clinically sound, and it looked as if she was an empathic practitioner. Was there something else going on with her?

Yet another thing he didn't have time for.

Stefan took a deep breath and pushed aside the horrible thought. Paige seemed to have gone into overdrive. She was giving orders and checking patients. He pulled his ski equipment on again. Even in bad weather, he was confident he could reach the alcove part way up the road where he'd parked his car early this morning. It wasn't far on foot. It should only take five minutes to drive up to the hospital to open it up and ensure he'd be ready to host these patients.

When he turned back, Paige was standing behind him in her bright red gear, and a pink hat that she'd obviously borrowed from someone else.

'I'll head up. I should be back in half an hour. You decide which patient we should move first. Either Lynn or Joe will need to come up with the first patient, so they can stay with them in the hospital while we transfer the rest.'

She raised her eyebrows. 'I've already decided which patient should come first and left instructions.'

'You're not coming with me,' he said steadily, seeing the glint of determination in her eyes.

'Yes, I am,' she said with equal force. 'You're not going up alone.'

Stefan felt his skin prickle. It was the way she was looking at him. It was setting off charges that hadn't been alive in…

'It's not sensible for both doctors to leave together. If something happened to both of us on the way up the mountain, who would look after these patients?'

She pressed her lips tightly together. He knew it made sense. And so did she.

'Okay,' she said finally, then lowered her voice. 'But don't think you'll win on everything. It might be your hospital, but this is an emergency situation. And we're equal partners here.'

There was a grim determination to her voice, an edge to her, that he hadn't seen before.

And it sparked his curiosity even more. Who was this woman, and why on earth did she intrigue him in ways he hadn't felt in…for ever?

CHAPTER FOUR

THE TRANSFERS WERE smoother than expected. It wasn't easy taking one patient at a time, climbing over snow to reach Stefan's four-by-four, then taking them up to a half-renovated hospital. But they got into a rhythm.

Between herself, Stefan, Joe, Lynn and Cathy, they managed to work out a way to keep all the patients safe. Whilst the hospital was surrounded by snow, the top part of the road was clear and the building was completely undamaged.

Her first sight of it took her breath away. The outside was beautiful and imposing. While parts of the building looked original, including some delicate stained-glass panes at the entrance and some old-fashioned stone pillars and steps leading up to impressive doors, the rest of the front of the building had clearly had a complete overall. It meant that the front had a pale stone façade, with brand-new windows. It looked like a prestigious and impressive place to be treated.

Stefan had quickly ensured all power and water supplies were working before showing them the main patient suites, which were already set up. All they had to do was make up the beds with the linens already stored in the closets. She was impressed by the way he swept around the place and his attention to detail. Every now and then he caught her gaze and held it for a moment longer than expected. She wondered what might have happened if it had been a normal day and their sparky conversation had continued in the café. Might it have led to drinks? To dinner?

It was clear he was frustrated that the place wasn't finished, and she wondered what Stefan the surgeon would be like to work with. She imagined he would have exacting standards about everything—the arrogance of surgeons always made her smile. In the frantic environment of A&E she'd seen a few cut down to size, and she wondered how he would have fared in her Glasgow department.

Paige gave herself a shake. She was too interested in this guy by far. She needed to get a message to her family to let them know she was safe, and she had patients to treat.

He showed them where the rest of the deliveries had arrived. There were boxes and boxes, it looked like medical sundries and supplies, all of which would be needed but could be examined and unpacked once all the patients were comfortable. Joe had already found a locked delivery of medicines for immediate use.

By the time the last patient had arrived, Paige was waiting outside for Stefan, still in her ski jacket.

'What's wrong?' he queried.

She could tell he was tired, and ready to get inside and get warm.

'One last trip,' she said. 'Down to the chalet so we can collect some food. It shouldn't take too long.'

Recognition sparked in his eyes. 'Of course.' He sighed. 'I'd forgotten about the food.'

'That's why you have me,' she said with a smile as he turned the car around and headed down the dark, twisting road.

'Think our nurses and physio will be okay?'

'I think they'll be great,' answered Paige sincerely. 'They seem so switched on. You were lucky some of the medical supplies had arrived and you were able to give some pain relief.'

He shook his head as he drove. 'I actually can't believe how lucky that was. We need to do X-rays, other tests, probably some surgery. But I'm hoping the pain relief will let a few of our patients get settled and over the shock of all this.'

Paige swallowed and breathed. 'Well, if you find a magic wand to get over the shock of all this, can you wave it over me too? I keep thinking I'll wake up in that really comfortable bed and realise this has all just been some crazy dream.'

He gave her a curious look. 'If only,' he said in a voice that was heavy and regretful. 'This couldn't have happened at a worse time.'

She turned her head and looked at him, about to query the comment. But of course, his new business was about to open. 'Hopefully it won't delay things for too long,' she said in an attempt at some kind of comfort.

But Stefan shook his head. 'It's more the knock-on effects of everything else. The clinic opening late also delays my other plans for the patients I have through Médecins Sans Frontières. We'd planned for twelve surgeries this year. I hate the thought of a child having to wait for surgery because of things that are out of my control.'

'You work for Médecins Sans Frontières?'

He nodded. 'I do two spells for them a year, and then the surgeries for children—mainly those with cleft lip and palate. The surgeries for cleft lip and palate need to be done in order, and they're complicated. Delays can impact on a child's eating, or in a developmental delay of their speech. I hate for any to fall behind.'

She looked at him carefully. 'Between here, Hollywood and your other work, you lead a pretty busy life. Do you ever have a break?'

'Do you?' The words came out instantly and his head whipped around to glance at her, before turning back to the road.

Paige pressed her lips together. She'd clearly struck a nerve. Maybe others had mentioned something to him too.

After her experiences in the last few months, should she be nervous driving back to the isolated chalet with a guy she barely knew? Maybe she should. But all her instincts around this guy in the last few hours were good. He was dedicated, and caring. He certainly seemed to work hard. But there was more than that. Rather than just considering her safety, she was actually quite curious about him. Who was Stefan Bachmann? She'd barely scratched the surface.

The drive was less than five minutes and Paige quickly put in the code to open the chalet door and showed Stefan into the kitchen. Thoughts could wait, they had priorities right now. She opened the fridge. 'We have everything in here.' She pointed to the welcome hamper. 'We have this.' Then she walked over to the large larder cupboard. 'And everything in here.'

Stefan's eyes widened as he noticed the supplies. He walked over and looked at her. 'Pasta, soup, tins, rice, flour, sugar. You've certainly got this stocked as if you expected to be stranded.'

He was looking at her in a curious way and she realised he'd never actually asked her if this place was hers. She was suddenly very self-conscious. Did she look like the kind of person who could own a place like this?

'Not me,' she said quickly. 'I'm only a temporary resident. But the owner seems to have thought of everything to keep people comfortable—even though I don't think he ever stays here.'

'Who does own this place?'

Paige took a breath, suddenly unsure of what to say. But they were in the middle of a disaster. Surely it wouldn't matter.

'I think they like to keep it quiet.' She named the well-known baron.

Stefan let out a low whistle in surprise. The baron was pretty notorious worldwide.

Paige was quick to jump in. 'Apparently he has places like this all over the world and he lets people like me use them. Health staff who need a holiday. And others, I think, who need some respite.' She tilted her head to the side and looked at Stefan. 'Maybe a bit like what you mentioned about your hospital. Some place out of the way, where people can get some privacy and a chance to relax. He just likes to keep things quiet.'

Stefan rolled his eyes. 'Well, this place is definitely relaxing in luxury.'

'And just for that,' said Paige, 'I won't show you the ski equipment cupboard that residents are free to use.' Something jolted in her brain. She had no idea where the very expensive skis and ski poles were she'd left with this morning. 'Darn it. I might have lost some of it.' She licked her lips and blew out a long breath. 'Okay, I'll send an email when we get back to the hospital, letting the owner know that I've emptied the store cupboard and—' she pulled a face '—likely misplaced some ski equipment.'

She pulled open a drawer she'd found earlier. 'Here. There's some bags you can use to transport the food out to the car. I'm going to nip upstairs and grab some of my clothes so Cathy and Lynn have some spares.'

Stefan nodded and by the time she came back down it was clear he'd made numerous trips to the car already. As he came back through the main door in a blast of icy air she could see the lines around his eyes. She looked at him and was thoughtful for a moment before gesturing to him and pulling open the ski equipment store.

'Listen, there's some extra ski jackets in here. Boots too. Do you want some for yourself and Joe?'

'You're offering me a ski jacket from Baron Boastful?'

Paige frowned and pulled a face. 'It's interesting that's his nickname, isn't it? When my experience is entirely the opposite. He doesn't want anyone to know he consistently does good deeds like this.'

'Maybe it's a tax dodge,' said Stefan over his shoulder as he walked back to the kitchen to grab more supplies.

'You're such a cynic.' She closed the door on the equipment store. 'That'll be a no, then?'

Stefan walked past, his arms loaded. 'I think we're taking enough of his stuff. Both Joe and I already have jackets. We'll dry them well enough, and hopefully be able to stay inside until the road's cleared.'

As he smiled she noticed how his eyes creased. He'd been surprisingly good company. She liked his occasional teasing, and the way he didn't take himself too seriously. He clearly didn't shy away from hard work either. She remembered the athletic build of the man she'd seen on the ski slope before their meeting at the café, and she tried to push it aside. Now wasn't the time to think like that.

They packed up the car and made their way back to the hospital. The lights were bright and it seemed more welcoming now. Stefan backed the car up so it would be easier to unload. The surrounding area was dark, and as they stepped out of the car a sharp gust of wind nearly blew her off her feet. She grabbed onto the car again. 'Whoa!'

He moved around beside her and put his arm around her waist and ducked his head down as they pushed through the door. The others were close by and came over at their arrival.

'Everyone okay?' asked Stefan immediately.

Joe nodded. 'Need some help?'

'Be careful out there, everyone,' said Paige quickly. 'The winds are still dreadful.'

Cathy zipped up her jacket. 'Once we've got the food, we can close up and stay inside. Depending what food we have, Lynn and I will try and pull something together, so we can feed everyone before they get to sleep.' She turned to them both. 'We'll give you a rundown on them all, but all are settled with their painkillers. Why don't we leave any casts or surgeries until the morning, when we're all over the shock of what's happened?'

Stefan gave a slow nod. 'Franco gave me a radio. We can get back in touch to find out if they've made contact with emergency services. It might be we can get everyone out of here in the next few hours. As long as everyone is comfortable, I'd rather not start anything, if that's an option.'

They all nodded and, after a few trips out to the car, deposited the food in the kitchen.

Lynn looked at them both. 'You two are freezing. As you can tell, the heating is working, so is the hot water. Go and grab a shower while I make a meal.'

Paige looked around. 'I'll show you,' said Stefan quietly, clearly realising she hadn't quite got her bearings yet.

He took her down a corridor and they both stuck their heads in the rooms, saying hello to their patients to make sure all were fine.

Although the rooms had really been designed for one patient each, because there was space for private staff, two or three had been put in each room. Cathy, and Lynn and Joe had taken other rooms, leaving one last suite.

Stefan clearly realised this and looked awkwardly at her. 'Do you want to bunk in with Cathy?'

It made sense, of course it did. But she didn't know Cathy any better than she knew Stefan. 'Why don't we worry about that later? Just show me a bathroom with a working shower and let me find some clean clothes.'

She dumped her bag on a nearby chair, trying to hide her surprise at the size of the suite. It had the largest hospital bed she'd ever seen, clearly with all modern accoutrements. The floor was some kind of luxury vinyl, easy to clean, but as she pulled off her boots and socks she realised it was warm and oddly soft underfoot.

Blinds had been pulled over the large windows, and there was an array of other doors leading off the main room.

Stefan had walked through one and she could hear running water and see the visible steam drifting out through the door already. Bliss. She couldn't wait.

There was a pile of bed linen sitting on another chair, along with towels and bathrobes.

Stefan stepped out. 'All yours.' He looked down at the pile she was looking at and waved his hand. 'There are two other rooms for staff and private nurses. I'll make up the beds, you grab a towel and go ahead.'

She considered pausing and offering to help, but was exhausted and felt grimy. 'Thanks,' she said, taking her clothes with her and heading into the bathroom.

Like everything else in this place, it was luxurious, with pristine white sanitary ware and gleaming gold taps. The mirror was already steamed up, and Paige sat her towel and fresh clothes near the basin and stripped off her clothes.

As her bright red and now grimy salopettes dropped to the floor she realised how little she'd been prepared for today as she'd hit the slopes. Her thermals and other clothes soon joined the pile on the floor and she stepped under the streaming warm water. It was bliss, heating her chilled skin instantly. She looked around for some soap or shower gel, but it seemed that those extras hadn't been found yet. It didn't matter, she was happy enough just to rub her face and body with her hands. After a few seconds' contemplation, she pulled her hair from the ponytail and let the water stream over her hair too. If no hairdryers existed, she could just tie it back up.

Ten minutes later she'd dried herself and pulled on her clean clothes—fresh underwear, a pair of jeans and a pink T-shirt. It was such a relief. She gathered her dirty clothes and towel and headed back out—and stopped.

Stefan was sitting on top of the bed. He'd removed his boots and jacket but was still wearing all his layers. His head had sagged forward with his chin resting on his chest. Was that a tiny snore?

She froze, not wanting to disturb him.

After a few moments she bit her lip. She couldn't stay here with a pile of dirty linen in her hands. Her stomach growled loudly and Stefan's head jerked up.

Paige started to laugh. She couldn't help it, particularly as her uncontrollable stomach decided to make yet another loud growl.

Stefan's eyes widened as he took in her position. Realisation flooded his eyes and he started laughing too. He pointed. 'Is that what woke me up, your stomach?'

Paige kept laughing as heat flooded her cheeks.

'How long have you been standing there?' he asked as he swung his legs off the bed.

'Hours,' she replied promptly, moving over to the bag she'd brought.

She saw the tiny flicker of panic. 'Minutes.' She waved her hand. 'Your turn for the shower and I'll go and claim one of the other bedrooms.'

She moved through to a very comfortable room with a hastily made bed. Hospital corners weren't Stefan's forte. She'd remember to tease him later.

Everything else in the room was great, including the small en suite bathroom she hadn't even considered might be there. She shook her head. In future she would take a shower in here, and she hung up one of the bathrobes on the hook behind the door.

She paused in the main room, wondering if she should wait for him. But it would be better to recheck all the patients and do whatever she could to help feed everyone. As she went to leave, the satellite phone lit up and she grabbed it, taking a few seconds to work out how to answer.

Franco's voice was a little patchy, but it was there.

'How is everyone?'

'Well, we're here. The electricity and heating are working, and I picked up some food from the chalet. Stefan wondered if there was any chance of transport, before we start any procedures on the patients.'

'Yeah, about that…' Franco paused and she heard a huge sigh.

'What's wrong?'

'Obviously, it's night-time now and difficult to make a full assessment. But the avalanche and landslide has completely blocked the road. They can't get a helicopter in the sky to get a proper look at the damage, due to the high winds. Bad news is, the winds are due to get worse—they think it might not be safe to get a helicopter up for the next few days.'

Her heart sank. 'So we could be stuck here for days?'

Franco cleared his throat, and there was a pause. 'We could be.'

Panic prickled Paige's skin. She licked her dry lips. It took a moment for her to collect her thoughts and ask the question she should. 'Is everyone who stayed with you still okay?'

'Yes,' Franco replied quickly. 'All good. We'll just need to get comfortable and wait.'

'So, I guess we'd better go ahead with the X-rays and treatments,' she said, more to herself than Franco. Her stomach was twisting and it was nothing to do with being hungry. It was dread. Fatigue. Worry.

'Yes, I'll get back to you once I speak to the authorities in the morning. They'll likely be in touch to see if you require any medical supplies.'

'Okay, thank you.'

She ended the call and leaned against the wall, breathing, trying to stop her heart racing in her chest. She couldn't quite understand why she was reacting this way. Paige had never been a panicker. Always managed in a crisis at work. Kept a cool head.

'What's wrong?'

She spun around as she heard his voice. Stefan was standing in the doorway of the bathroom, a towel around his hips.

Her mouth fell open. He was lean and muscular, with defined biceps and dark hair scattering his chest. He seemed completely comfortable with the fact he wasn't wearing much.

He looked down. 'Sorry, forgot to grab other clothes. I have a rucksack I left here yesterday. It has some spare clothes, and I think there might be scrubs along at the theatres.'

Paige was having trouble constructing words.

'What's wrong?' he asked again, moving over to the bed and picking up another bathrobe that was lying there.

For a moment she wondered if the towel might drop while he put the bathrobe on, but no, of course not. He slid the bathrobe on, tied it at the waist, then tugged the towel from underneath. Perfectly covered. She wasn't sure she liked it.

'Paige?'

Her brain seemed to have a jolt of recovery. She held up the phone. 'We could be stuck here for a few days. Weather is closing in and it's unlikely any helicopters will be able to fly and get our casualties out.'

'Darn it,' and he muttered something else under his breath.

'We'll need to treat everyone.' The words came out with a slight tremor to them that she couldn't explain.

He nodded. 'Let's check everyone. We can decide if we need to do anything immediately. If it's safe, we'll let them eat, ensure they are pain free and get a good night's rest. I want to double-check what equipment, tools and drugs we have before we start.'

Paige raised her eyebrows. 'And you need some clothes,' she added.

He sighed, looking down at his white robe. 'I can't go in this?'

She gave a laugh. 'I don't want to be responsible for what happens if that bathrobe accidentally opens.'

This time it was Stefan's eyes that rose in surprise. 'I'll keep that in mind. I'll meet you in the kitchen in five.'

Paige turned and walked down the corridor, half cringing at her careless comment. At a moment of natural disaster, was she flirting?

She shook her head as her stomach grumbled again. She put a hand on her stomach. 'I'll blame it on low blood sugar.' She smiled to herself as she tried to get the image of Stefan and his towel out of her head.

* * *

There was something slightly off about Paige. She looked good. She looked well. He was well aware that they'd been out in the cold for some time. It was likely that every patient and staff member here could have suffered an element of hypothermia, and letting everyone rest for a few hours would give them a chance to get warmed through. Could it just be that which was wrong with her?

There was so much he didn't know about this doc. He'd been shocked to see how slim she was, now that she'd shed all her skiwear. The bones around her neck and shoulders were prominent in her pink top, and was there a hint of a bruise too?

Of course, that might be developing after today's events. But his gut told him it was a little older and was fading instead of just emerging. He could remember having a similar thought at the café earlier.

He'd grabbed some underwear and pulled on a set of navy scrubs. It wasn't the warmest clothing, but the boiler had definitely kicked in and the temperature was rising gradually. The corridors were still cold, but each of the rooms was at a comfortable level of heat.

Lynn and Cathy had taken the eggs and bread that had come from the chalet and made scrambled eggs and toast for everyone. It was simple and not too heavy for bodies which had been under strain today.

The most worrisome patient was Rafe, the man who'd been buried deeply under the snow. He was on low level oxygen and had been given pain relief for his likely rib fractures. Cathy, the cardiac physio, had found an ultrasound machine. Whilst she was familiar with the technology for looking at hearts, she'd adapted and been able to show their pregnant woman who had cramping that there was a definite flickering heartbeat in her uterus and put her mind at rest. Eva had shed tears of relief and agreed to keep resting.

The newly flung-together staff were currently sitting in the kitchen, on stools at one of the preparation stations. They could have made it into the formal dining room, but it was distinctly lacking any furniture.

Joe came back along the corridor with a makeshift head injury chart he'd made on paper, a pen torch in his hand, and slid it in front of Paige. 'Bruno seems stable.' He gave a smile. 'But, as a theatre guy, conscious patients aren't really my forte.'

Stefan smiled. 'I'll be glad to have you tomorrow. And Lynn, thank goodness you work in orthopaedics. We'll have two ankles to maybe pin. A tib-fib fracture to sort, and an ulna and radius. All will need casts. All will need X-rays, as will our two people with likely fractured ribs.'

Joe nodded. 'Are you okay if I go for a look around your theatre, and your surgical equipment?'

'Absolutely. Some of the surgical packs arrived today. The monitors, operating tables and gas supplies are up and running in the theatres. At least that part of the renovations stayed on track.'

There was a nudge at his elbow. Paige had sat down next to him, a large steaming mug of hot chocolate in her hands. 'Did you tell them the rest?'

All eyes turned towards him.

Stefan sighed. 'Paige heard from Franco. Everyone is fine back at the café, but the weather forecast for the next few days is bad. It's unlikely helicopters will be able to get anyone out.'

'Or insulin in,' said Lynn sharply.

Paige looked at her, remembering Bob, their diabetic man who'd smashed his insulin pen. 'Do we have any at all?'

She nodded. 'Only short-acting. It's different to the one Bob usually uses, but will still work. But he takes a long-acting insulin every evening to give him a steady background of insulin throughout the day. We don't have any of that.'

Stefan nodded slowly. 'Does he have a glucose monitor? I know we have some in the treatment room.'

'He has a sensor which will last another five days.'

They all looked at each other.

'It will be Christmas before then.' Paige said the words that the rest of them had been skirting around.

Christmas Eve was in three days' time. The weather report made it sound as if it could be a strange kind of Christmas.

Paige swallowed and tilted her chin upwards with a look of determination on her face. 'Hopefully by then the road will be clear. If not, there's some Christmas decorations in the chalet we can bring up. We'll need to find some kind of presents for Claudia.'

The seven-year-old. What kind of a Christmas might that be for her? 'At least her mum is with her,' said Paige quickly.

'And there might be jigsaws or games at the chalet we can use.'

The rest looked sombre but nodded. Stefan stood up. 'You guys get some sleep. I'm going to check everyone over and make sure the buzzer system works so they can let us know if they need anything during the night.'

'I'll help.' Paige stood quickly.

Cathy rubbed her eyes. 'Thanks, guys. I can't wait to get to sleep.'

Paige walked alongside him as they checked everyone over. She borrowed a stethoscope and listened to Rafe's chest again. Broken ribs were always tricky. There wasn't a way to magically heal them or make them completely pain-free. The act of breathing alone meant that Rafe's ribs were moving. Trouble was, they really needed him to breathe deeply to avoid pneumonia.

Paige's expression was grave as she pulled back.

'Can I get you some more pain relief?'

Rafe gave a nod and she scribbled something on the makeshift chart beside his bed, and came back a few moments later with some tablets and a glass of water.

Stefan ensured he was as comfortable

as possible and had his buzzer before they started the long walk down the corridor.

Paige stopped at the main entrance, running her fingers over the stained glass. 'Do you know anything about this?' she asked.

He stopped beside her. The sharpness and sparkiness he'd seen last night and this morning had drained out of her. For the last few hours, he'd caught himself looking at her and wondering why, at times, her dark eyes looked haunted.

He spoke quietly. 'I do. It wasn't here originally. It was made by one of the first prisoners of war that stayed here for a while. He made a recovery and learned how to make stained glass. He made the two panels, one with the Turaco, the national bird of Switzerland, and one with the Swiss flag, as part of a thank you.'

She traced her fingers over the glass. 'I've never heard of a Turaco before—or seen one. The colours are beautiful.'

The colours were startling—green, purple, blue and a tiny bit of red.

He nodded. 'They are really only found in Switzerland or South Africa. Aren't they amazing?'

'It looks like it should live somewhere tropical. How did it find its way to the Alps?'

Stefan shook his head. He could sense her starting to relax a little, her shoulders dropping slightly, the clench around her jaw easing. She really was incredibly attractive and he was trying not to be distracted. 'I have no idea. I've never asked. To be honest, I'd forgotten these were here.'

She turned around and stared at him. 'How many times have you walked past these in the last few months?'

It was a fair question. He opened his mouth to try and give some kind of excuse, but they all just seemed so lame that he couldn't actually find the words.

She spoke for him. 'Too busy? Not enough time to stop and take a look?'

His mouth felt dry. All of a sudden, the events of the day seemed to flood his body. He was tired—beyond tired. His brain was still churning. It couldn't switch off, planning surgeries for tomorrow, thinking of potential complications for any of his current patients. And he was wondering how long it would take to clear the road. It wouldn't be safe to bring diggers up in bad weather to try and move the debris. Their best chance was a helicopter. But the weather forecast was bad.

'Stefan?' Paige had stepped forward and

had her hand on his arm. The heat from her fingertips sent a world of sensations across his skin. 'I'm sorry. I didn't mean to offend you.'

He put his hand on hers. It was instinctive. 'You didn't,' he said gently. 'But you might have hit a nerve,' he admitted.

Neither of them had moved their hands. Something stirred deep inside him. A connection. What was it about this woman?

He looked at the stained glass. 'You're right. It is beautiful. And my great-grandmother told my gran about them. She'd left by the time they were put in place, but she'd looked after the man who made them.'

'Wow. That's a real piece of history.'

He turned to her. 'Want to see more history?'

He was feeling guilty—guilty about all the times he hadn't slowed down to take a breath. To appreciate things like this.

Paige looked curious. 'Yes, of course.'

He had a strange urge to grab her hand, but knew that wouldn't be entirely appropriate. 'Come with me,' he said instead, and led her down the corridor, grabbing keys from the main office, along with a couple of jackets.

She stared at the dirty but bright yellow and orange jacket he handed her.

'It'll be cold. These must belong to the workmen. Better to put something over your T-shirt.' He grabbed two torches and took her down a dimly lit corridor on the opposite side of the building.

The drop in temperature was instantly noticeable and Paige shivered and wrapped her arms around herself. 'I've never been so glad for heating.'

He nodded. 'The pipes have been put in, but there's still too much to do over here—the electrics, the walls, all the renovations—and it means there's no heating here yet. He came to a set of double doors with panes of glass in the top half. He turned a key and pushed one open with a loud creak.

'This is really the best-kept secret. It should have been torn out a few weeks ago. But with the delays, the workmen just hadn't reached it yet.'

He lifted his hand and let his torchlight sweep over the room. Paige gave a loud gasp.

It was an old traditional ward, with a wooden floor and high hospital beds lined up on either side of the room, next to the dark windows. It was like a hundred black and white photographs that she had seen in textbooks. Or a scene from a historical movie.

He wondered if she would be scared. But, before he could say anything, Paige had switched on her own torch and moved over to the nearest bed, touching the bottom of it. 'Just think of the people,' she whispered. 'Think of the stories. Think of the lives… and deaths.' She moved to the next bed then spun around, letting her light strobe up and down the other side of the room. 'What about all the men who were sent here? I wonder if they were all relieved, or whether some of them were angry about not being able to fight any more.'

This had been a purely instinctive thing—to show her this part of the hospital. And it could have gone horribly wrong. It might have scared her. Or just not interested her at all.

But Paige's face was full of wonder. He could virtually see her brain contemplating the possibilities. Thinking about all the history from years gone by.

All the things he hadn't really had time to consider.

His skin prickled again, but not in the way it had earlier. This time he was uncomfortable.

'I've never really thought about it,' he admitted.

'Your great-grandmother must have had a million stories about this place. The people. The patients. The medicine.' She smiled as she looked at him and he gave a sad shrug.

'I never got to have those conversations. And my gran could remember a few things, but not any of the details. She knew her parents had met here but, like many others of their time, it seemed like my great-grandparents didn't want to talk about the war much. They'd lived it. They didn't want to remember it.'

Paige visibly shivered again. 'Thank you,' she said sincerely. 'Thank you for showing me this place. If we get a chance tomorrow, I'd like to come back and see it in the daylight.'

He nodded and moved back to the double doors. 'The keys will be in the office. They're yours to take any time you want to.'

Her smile was soft. 'Thanks.' She looked down at her dirty workman's jacket and laughed. 'Free use of the jacket too?'

'Absolutely,' he said with a laugh as he locked the doors behind them.

As they walked back down the corridor the heat enveloped them again. All of a sudden the corridor seemed very long. They had the last room, at the very far end. Stefan was conscious they hadn't really had a chance to talk about sharing a suite.

'Do you want me to sleep someplace else?' he asked.

Paige stopped walking and looked at him. 'No, of course not. Why would you ask that?'

He waved his hand towards their suite. 'We were last here. All the other suites had already been taken. I wonder if Cathy, Joe and Lynn wondered if perhaps we were here together, and that's why they left that last place for us.'

'What?' Paige's mouth fell open and her brow furrowed, then she started to nod and her hand came up to her mouth. 'Oh, my. They met us together. It hadn't even occurred to me they might think that.' She started to laugh.

'Am I that bad?' Stefan joked.

'Well, I don't know that yet, do I?' she quipped. 'But seriously, we have separate rooms in there. And I'm sorry for hogging the bathroom earlier. I didn't realise I had a separate shower in the en suite.'

'Don't be silly. It's fine, and those rooms are much smaller, so are the bathrooms.'

Paige nodded. 'I seriously need to find some toiletries.'

'Me too. There are probably boxes somewhere with all those tiny bottles of things that people usually get in hotels. We've just not had cause to put them out yet.'

They looked at each other. 'Tomorrow?'

Then laughed at their simultaneous question.

'I need to sleep,' sighed Paige.

'Me too,' said Stefan.

'We'll definitely hear if one of the buzzers goes off?'

He nodded. 'But we'll need to keep our doors open. So you may well also hear me snore.'

She waved her hand. 'I can probably snore louder. So don't worry.'

She turned back to head to her room, and then stopped and looked over her shoulder. 'Thank you.' Her voice was quiet.

Stefan was confused. 'What for?'

'Being here,' she said, her voice a little shaky, before she disappeared into her room.

CHAPTER FIVE

WHILST THE BED was comfortable, it wasn't the best night's sleep. The wind howled and the trees nearby creaked, making her wonder if they might come down on the hospital. The buzzers went a few times, mainly just for minor things, but the disturbed sleep didn't help.

By the time she'd showered in the morning and dressed in a pair of scrubs, Paige felt as if she'd done ten rounds in a boxing ring. New bruises had appeared on her body—clearly from where she'd fallen with Stefan in the café to shelter.

Strange things were happening with her. Yesterday on a few occasions she'd felt an unusual connection with Stefan. Paige had only had a few relationships— things she'd kind of fallen into. But she'd never really met someone and felt an instant attraction—a buzz—and she part wondered if she was just stressed and this was her brain trying to distract her.

But her brain couldn't make up the little flutter in her chest when her eyes sometimes connected with Stefan's, or the tingle in her fingers when her skin had come into contact with his.

Her life felt like a rollercoaster. One day she'd been at work, then she'd been sent on a recuperation holiday of a lifetime, then she'd been involved in a natural disaster, which now meant she was trapped. If she told someone this story it was likely they wouldn't believe her.

She'd never felt so unsettled. So uncertain or so unsure. This whole situation was madness. But, hopefully, manageable madness. In her head she had already formed a list. X-rays. Assessment. Surgeries. Theatre was not normal for an A&E doctor, but sometimes she'd been called to assist, or ended up in situations in the resus room that weren't too far from theatre procedures. She might need some guidance but she was confident enough that she could assist Stefan.

But all that still couldn't explain that tiny feeling in the pit of her stomach. It had been there for a long time, but coming here had finally forced her to acknowledge it. She might be in the middle of a disaster, but things were stripped back here. She didn't have her own job to think about. She wasn't surrounded by familiar things and friends. Taking those parts of her life away and realising the gnawing feeling was still there made it all the more real.

She walked down the corridor to the kitchen. The sun wasn't up entirely, but all her colleagues were. Tea was made, and a large box of cornflakes and a stack of bowls sat on the counter.

'Don't want to torture people with the smell of toast if we have to fast them for surgery,' said Lynn. 'That would just be mean.'

She pushed the milk towards Paige, who filled her bowl. 'Do we know how we're starting?'

Stefan pushed a list towards her. 'This is the order I think we should do the X-rays. Do you agree?'

She glanced at it and nodded. 'Once we've reviewed, we'll decide the order for surgery or casts?'

The mood was sombre this morning, probably because they were all aware of the storm raging all night. Lynn handed over some charts. 'I decided to formalise our paperwork. Observations, medicines and notes. Found a computer and printer in the office—' she smiled at Stefan '—that thankfully had the generic log-in on a sticky note next to it.'

He rolled his eyes. 'My colleague was site manager here. He's notorious at work for it. Fortunately for him, his wife is expecting twins and he had to fly back to Hollywood at short notice.' He looked up at the ceiling and shook his head. 'You have no idea how glad I am that he wasn't here when this happened.'

They all nodded. Stefan sighed. 'I've checked everyone this morning. Given some more pain meds so we can move to X-ray. There were a few tears. I think shock is finally hitting our patients. Yesterday, they were just grateful to have survived, and to have somewhere warm to sleep. Today, they are stiff and sore from yesterday, and most of them have clocked the weather and know it's likely we'll be here for a few days. Christmas is a big issue.'

'If it comes to it, we can make Christmas work,' said Paige decisively.

'Has anyone spoken to Franco yet this morning?'

They all shook their heads. 'Let's do some X-rays,' said Joe. 'Hopefully by the time we're finished, Franco might have some news for us.'

Ninety minutes later, Stefan and Paige had all the information they needed. Little Claudia definitely needed surgery to pin her tibia and fibula. One of the women with a fractured ankle needed some manipulation and a cast. The other needed surgery, as did the woman with the fractured ulna and radius. Rafe had six rib fractures. He was probably the sickest here, but there was no surgery that could help him. Bruno's head injury was stable, but he still needed observation. Eva, the pregnant lady, was fine, just anxious, and Bob was keeping his blood sugar under control with only the short-acting insulin. The one who was giving unexpected concern was their elderly man with angina. After a comfortable night, settled with some nitrate medicine, Eduardo had started to experience chest pain again. His ECG was mildly concerning.

'In an ideal world we would do emergency bloods,' said Paige. 'But there's no chance of that here.'

Stefan looked around. It was clear he was measuring the range of experience in the room. 'I know the weather isn't good,' he said carefully. 'But, if there's a break in the weather, we might have a chance to Medevac some people out. Eduardo would be my number one patient to get out of here. He needs bloods, and probably somewhere they have a cath lab in case he's heading for a myocardial infarction. Does everyone agree?'

Paige nodded. 'Who would you consider next?'

'That's difficult,' he mused. 'It could depend on how our surgeries go today. If we could get extra insulin for Bob, he will be fine. If Bruno took a turn for the worse, I'd struggle with the appropriate surgical equipment, or the expertise. He'd be next for me.'

Paige nodded again. 'It's like playing a lottery with people's lives, and I hate that. But we have to try and prioritise.' They'd already decided that both doctors and Joe would be in Theatre today. Lynn would do any casts post-surgery, and Cathy would be keeping an eye on everyone else.

Cathy gave a solemn nod. 'So, if Franco gets in touch, I know the first two patients to get ready for transfer.'

'Don't be afraid to come and get us. Getting someone inside a rescue stretcher is difficult. They might only send the stretcher down in a winch if they think it's too dangerous to send the member of staff. It will likely be based on timing. So come and tell us if you need to.'

Paige's thoughts were circulating back to experiences she'd rather forget. 'I can help,' she said quietly. 'I'm familiar with the stretcher and winch technology. We've transferred a number of patients via the roof of the hospital before.'

Stefan gave a grateful nod. 'Fantastic. Been a while since I've been near one.'

'You've used them too?'

He nodded. 'When I first went to California I was based near Long Beach. Had a short-term role with air and sea rescue.'

Paige was intrigued. Stefan had made a comment last night about being busy. Did the guy ever stop working?

'That's great.' She stood up and stretched her back. 'Are we ready to get started?'

Everyone nodded.

Paige was nervous. Operating theatres were a little outside her comfort zone, but she could see that Stefan was right at home. He moved about with ease. Checking all the surgical tools that were ready. Moving the mobile X-ray machine and checking the drugs on a nearby tray. When he was finally happy he turned to them both. 'Lynn has Claudia and her mum outside. I'll give Claudia some light sedation before I bring her through. Joe, are you happy to monitor her, while I scrub?'

Joe nodded. He had years of experience in Theatre and had a specialist position as an advanced nurse who could also assist in anaesthetics. In the worst possible set of circumstances, it seemed that luck had smiled on them.

Things went smoothly. Claudia had an open reduction and internal fixation of her bones, and a cast applied. After everyone was content, they continued with their other surgeries. Frances had an open reduction and internal fixation of her ulna and radius. Anna required a pin in her ankle, and Greta was luckiest, with her bones still in position, and just required a plaster cast on her lower leg.

Stefan had been cool. He'd admitted reading up on all the surgeries last night—to refresh his brain. Paige was glad to hear him say that. She'd assisted as best she could, conscious of the fact that she would never have managed any of this on her own. He'd been thoughtful and respectful of them all—not like some of the arrogant surgeons she'd met in the past, and she was grateful, because her nerves could have got the better of her. But working alongside someone who was clearly careful and supportive had made her feel much more at ease.

She'd just pulled the pale pink cap from her head when Cathy rushed in. 'You were right. Franco just radioed. There might only be time to get one person out. They have a temporary break in the weather.'

Within five minutes Paige was outside, jacket over her theatre scrubs at a wide space in the middle of the car park. Poor Eduardo was behind a set of doors, ready to be bundled out and into the rescue stretcher.

The *thud-thud* of the helicopter sounded in the distance. The clouds above were thick and heavy and, from ground level, visibility was poor. Stefan had the satellite phone in his hand, listening to instructions. He gave a hand signal to Paige. Three minutes. She nodded. Bruno was also in the background, waiting to see if there would be a chance to evacuate two patients instead of one.

Paige was trying to pretend her heart wasn't thudding in her chest. She breathed in the freezing air and blew it out slowly, trying to count in her head. Anything to calm her nerves down. As the whirring increased above them, the dark body of the helicopter appeared. The side door opened and a man's legs swung over the edge, clearly operating the bright orange stretcher that descended towards them. There was also a small bag attached. Paige untied it with shaking fingers, as Stefan detached the stretcher. Paige could see Cathy talking directly into Eduardo's ear, trying to keep him calm. She wheeled him out and, between the three of them, they manoeuvred him into the stretcher, unable to talk properly because of the noise overhead. Eduardo had his hands across his chest, his GTN spray held tightly in one fist. Paige didn't even want to consider how scary this might be for a man with chest pain. Stefan had given him something to relax him in preparation. But would it work?

As they snapped the last clip into place, Paige gave the signal to ascend. The wind seemed to be picking up, or was it just the backdraught from the rotors above? The stretcher swung perilously as it started to move upwards to the helicopter. But that was normal. Paige knew from experience that the ascent was never in a straight line. How could it be?

Within moments, the operator above had grabbed the stretcher and loaded it on board. There were a few seconds' pause. It was clear the pilot and operator were discussing whether they had time to retrieve another patient. The operator gave a signal. Four minutes. They only had four minutes left.

A second stretcher descended and Stefan sprinted across the car park to the doors for Bruno. Every moment counted. He ran across with Bruno in the wheelchair. Bruno was well wrapped up, and easier to get into the stretcher than Eduardo had been. Within a few minutes the stretcher lifted into the sky, was bundled into the helicopter, the sliding door slammed shut and the helicopter disappeared into the dark clouds above.

It was bitterly cold. But Paige was momentarily frozen to the spot. Stefan bent down at her feet and grabbed the bag, which was still there. He caught her hand and pulled her back towards the hospital, slamming the doors behind them.

Cathy was already inside, tugging off her woolly hat. 'I think we made that by the skin of our teeth,' she said. Then she looked at them both, and obviously caught the expression on Paige's face. 'Kitchen,' she said bluntly. 'I'll make the tea.'

She turned and walked away while Stefan looked at Paige. 'You okay?'

She nodded and swallowed. 'Just absolutely freezing.' She hugged herself in her ski jacket. 'Didn't have time to dress properly underneath. And the noise from the helicopter made it difficult to concentrate. I didn't have a clue what I was doing out there.'

Stefan looked at her steadily. 'You manoeuvred two patients into a complicated stretcher system and ensured they were safe in a limited time frame. You did fine.' He held up the bag. 'Now, let's hope we've got some insulin in here.'

The bag was small, but thick and heavy. They opened it in the kitchen and found well-packaged insulin—both brands that Bob usually used, along with a new fourteen-day sensor. There were also some other drugs, another satellite phone, and some additional items.

Stefan stared at the phone for a few moments. 'Guess they think we might not be getting out of here soon.' He undid the wrapper on something else and frowned. 'What's this?'

Paige inspected the box. It was clearly something electronic. 'I think it might be a booster,' she said as she stared at one of the wires coming off it. 'Maybe to give us some kind of internet provision?'

'We've had barely anything since the avalanche,' said Cathy. 'It might help a lot. If some of our patients could contact their families they might be a bit more settled.'

Joe and Lynn came in. 'All patients that are left are fine.' He glanced at the items on the worktop. 'Oh, insulin, great. I'll take that along to Bob and put the rest in the medicine fridge.'

Lynn stayed near the doorway. She seemed to be reluctant to talk.

'What's wrong?' asked Paige.

Lynn sighed. 'Claudia's mum was quite tearful. Wondered why some people had been evacuated and not her and her child.'

Stefan straightened in his chair. 'We know why. The decision had to be made on a medical basis.'

Lynn shrugged. 'We know that. But they don't understand. Greta's upset too. They're stranded up a mountain after an avalanche, a few days before Christmas. People expect to be with their families at this time of year. It's hard. Particularly when we don't know what comes next.' She gave a soft smile. 'I'm lucky. I'm here with Joe. But if I was up here by myself I'd feel differently.'

Stefan ran his fingers through his hair. Paige could tell he was exasperated. 'I'll talk to them,' he said. 'I get that they're upset. But there has to be some perspective. We're all alive. We're all safe. We're somewhere warm, with electricity and food. We can survive. And people know that we're here. They will try and get us out.' He took a deep breath. 'I get that people are sentimental about Christmas. It's a time of year I love. If I don't get out of here, my dad will spend Christmas alone. But it's one day of the year. And he'll understand. He's a resilient old guy.' There was a real tinge of sadness to his words that struck somewhere deep down inside of Paige. She wanted to ask more. But now clearly wasn't the time.

She held up her hands. 'We can't control the weather. And we all have to take responsibility for the fact we knew there was a weather warning—albeit for the next day—and we still chose to go skiing. I had planned to head down to the town, get some more supplies, and spend the next few days holed up in the chalet. I would likely still have been stranded. But I would have been safe. I would have been warm and comfortable. Just like I am here.'

'You could go back to the chalet if you wanted,' said Stefan, his blue eyes connecting with hers. 'The rest of us don't have someplace else to go. But, if you wanted to, you could go back. There's no obligation to stay.'

Her skin prickled at the back of her neck. Was he testing her? Did he want her to leave? She hated the way she instantly felt inside. As if she could grab the keys to the car, disappear down the mountain and hide in the luxury cabin.

Anyone would be a fool not to consider it.

And she hated herself. Because it did flash through her brain. The thought of not having to be a doctor. The thought of actually having the holiday she was supposed to have. Switching off from it all. Hiding in the chalet with the warm fire, the exquisite library and hugely comfortable bed.

She was a horrible, terrible person. She shouldn't have let even that fleeting thought enter her brain.

'There's no way I'm leaving. I'll only go back to the chalet when the road is clear again and we can all get out of here.'

Cathy gave a nod and poured the tea, but Stefan was looking at her carefully. 'You don't have to.' He cleared his throat and shifted uncomfortably in his chair. 'We've done all the surgeries that we need to. Everyone is stable.'

'If it wasn't so tricky, we could probably have taken everyone back to the café, so we were all together.' Joe and Lynn came back through the door at this point and sat down, picking up mugs of tea as they were poured.

Stefan shook his head. 'Not much point in that. At least we have beds here. And all the food from the chalet. I know the cafés have food, but I'm not sure how much. I'm sure it's much more comfortable in the hospital. We are as well waiting things out here.'

Joe nodded. 'My back is too old to sleep on a floor these days.'

It made perfect sense. And even though Paige had been prepared to spend Christmas alone, she didn't mind being surrounded by other people.

She looked around at her colleagues and stood up. 'Why don't you let me cook this evening? We're all tired. I can make dinner and we can all try and get to bed early tonight.'

Joe, Lynn and Cathy all nodded in assent. Stefan looked at her. 'I'll help.'

She wasn't quite sure what to say. She'd wanted some space to think, but she could hardly turn down the offer of help.

'Of course,' she agreed in a tight voice.

The rest disappeared down the corridor,

likely to one of the other rooms to sit and relax.

Paige made her way over to where they'd placed all the provisions and pulled the cupboard doors open.

Stefan appeared at her elbow. 'Okay, so what dream dinner are you going to make?'

Paige looked around. 'I think it will be simple. Pasta, with a tomato sauce bulked by some of the vegetables while they are still fresh. We can toast some of the bread with garlic butter. Simple, but fine.'

He gave a nod and moved across the kitchen, lifting out a giant pot and filling it with water, and setting it on the hob. Paige grabbed some armfuls of packets and tins. She poured the pasta into the pot and handed him the tins. 'You open these tinned tomatoes and find another large pot. I'll chop all the vegetables.'

It wasn't quite as awkward as she had first thought. Stefan could find his way around the kitchen. He wasn't trying to interfere, just be helpful. After a few minutes, she could feel his eyes on her as she chopped the vegetables.

'Not doing it efficiently enough for you?' she joked. 'I would have given you this job, but didn't want to risk a surgeon's fingers.'

He gave a small smile but shot her a thoughtful glance. 'You did well today. I'm sorry if I didn't say it sooner.'

She looked at him in surprise. 'It was you that did well. You were doing orthopaedics. I know that's not normal for you.'

He shrugged. 'It's not. I usually deal with facial bones. But I have experience in other surgery, and have pinned and plated before, so it was just a case of remembering all I could.'

She kept chopping. 'You seemed confident.'

'I was pretending.'

She stopped and stared at him, kind of in shock. She gave him a sideways glance and started chopping again. 'Well, I guess I'll need to remember that about you. You're good at pretending.'

'You make me sound like some kind of spy.'

She raised her eyebrows. 'You could be. But, to be honest, if you were some kind of spy, I would have expected you to get us out of here today.'

'You mean, phone my headquarters and ask for the snow-burrowing machine to get through the road block?'

She wrinkled her nose. 'I was thinking

more high-tech.' She waved her knife as she spoke. 'You know, the machine that burrows to the centre of the earth, and then spins around and comes out just at the entrance-way to the hospital.'

'Oh, you wanted the big guns,' he joked.

She shrugged and put the onions and courgettes she'd chopped into the pan with the tomatoes, 'I did,' she admitted. 'But maybe you're not that level of spy.'

'You're dissing my spy status?'

'Of course.' She started combining ingredients to make the sauce.

He folded his arms. 'You seem pretty set on getting out of here.'

'Isn't everybody?'

She looked at him, because he hadn't replied. As she stirred the sauce she dug deeper. 'Are you telling me that you'd be happy to stay?'

Now he looked awkward. It was as if the handsome, broad-shouldered man had turned into a four-year-old boy who was shuffling his feet. 'Not…happy. Just not sad exactly either.'

She put down her wooden spoon. 'Okay, you've got me. I'm not touching this dinner until you tell me more.'

'You might get a bad review for your restaurant,' he quipped, clearly trying to change the subject again.

'Well, it's your restaurant, so see if I care.' She winked at him, and he burst out laughing.

He pointed his finger at her. 'So, there you are.'

He said it with satisfaction and she didn't quite get it. 'What do you mean?' She started stirring the sauce again.

'The girl I met in the café before the avalanche. The one that—how do you say it—wouldn't give me an inch?'

Now it was Paige's turn to shift uncomfortably. 'But I've been here all along.'

He leaned forward, putting both elbows on the counter and staring at her. 'But you weren't. You lost your spark.'

Paige was immediately on the defensive. 'Well, let me see, there was an avalanche, there were patients to treat. There were thoughts of being trapped and wondering what on earth happens next.'

Now, she was a bit annoyed. 'Anyhow, don't stand around doing nothing. Find the butter and the garlic, mix it up and put it on the bread. The oven is behind you.'

He raised his eyebrows. 'Bossy.'

Paige shook her head. 'Not at all. The

word you're looking for is direct, or I might even let you off with a Scottish word. Crabbit. That's what happens when you have to share a suite with a record-breaking snorer.'

Stefan's mouth fell open and he moved around the counter, coming up next to her. 'You can't get away with that one.' He picked up one of the wooden spoons and wagged it at her. 'You're the one that snores all night.'

'I do not,' she said, aghast. Or at least pretending to be. Her insides were cringing.

'You do so.'

'I'm going to tape you tonight. You literally start snoring the second you close your eyes. And even though there's a wall between us, I can still hear you.'

'Anyone would think you were criticising the renovations that have gone on here.'

'I wouldn't dare,' she sparked back. 'You might start charging me rent.'

Stefan started mixing the butter and pressed garlic together. He looked thoughtful. 'Now, that could actually be a good idea.'

Her phone buzzed and then started playing a tune. After a few seconds Stefan looked at her with his eyes wide. 'Really?'

She pulled her phone from the back pocket

of her jeans, letting the chorus of the eighties pop song 'Last Christmas' fill the air.

'Classic,' she said decidedly, prodding the pasta and deciding it was ready. 'Hurry up with that garlic bread.'

After all her earlier anxieties in the day she couldn't help but notice how relaxed she felt in Stefan's company. Somehow, just being around him, his easy chat and teasing manner seemed to lift her spirits and, as she watched, she wondered if she was having the same effect on him. The restlessness that seemed to plague him appeared to have been pushed away. It was nice just to concentrate on the moment.

He grabbed a knife and spread the garlic butter over the bread, lifting the tray and sliding it into the oven. 'No. You don't get to drop that Christmas tune without an explanation.' Then he looked at her curiously. 'Did you just get a signal on your phone?'

She sighed and pushed it towards him. 'I should be so lucky. No, it's a pre-set alarm.'

'What for?' It was a natural follow-up question, so Paige tried not to let it bother her.

'I take some supplements. It's just a reminder.'

He paused for a second then gave a brief

nod. 'And you need your favourite pop band of the eighties to remind you?'

Paige glanced in the pot. The sauce was definitely ready. 'Actually,' she said, as she drained the pasta, 'it's my favourite ever Christmas song. Has been for years. And I won't be moved on that.'

'"Last Christmas" is your favourite ever Christmas song?'

She nodded. 'Absolutely. Just be glad the weather is bad out there. I'd be out in that snow in a flash, trying to recreate the video.'

He rolled his eyes and shook his head. 'Who trapped me with an eighties fanatic?' he joked.

She stirred the sauce into the pasta. 'Actually, I have a whole host of Christmas songs on my phone. I might treat you to all my favourites if you're lucky.'

He started putting out plates for everyone. 'You just make this "snowed-in" event better by the moment.'

She sighed and looked around. 'I actually love Christmas. To be honest, the chalet was my dream come true. Christmas paraphernalia everywhere. A gorgeous setting. Lots of food. And the library. My plan was to spend all day playing "Last Christmas" and just mooching around.'

'Mooching?' He frowned.

She held up her hands. 'You know, flopping from one seat to another, going from room to room, being completely relaxed. I even brought my own advent calendar with me. A proper one. Not one filled with chocolate. You know, the kind you had as a kid, where you open a window each day and see a Christmas picture—a robin, a reindeer, a Christmas wreath, a present.' She stared spooning the dinner onto plates. 'You know, they're very hard to find these days.'

Stefan turned, grabbed some oven gloves and pulled the tray of garlic bread from the oven. 'What can I say?' He shrugged. 'I'm from Switzerland, the land of chocolate. I'm with the kids that like the chocolate advent calendar.'

'Primitive,' she joked as the warm aroma of the garlic bread surrounded them. 'Okay—' she put her hands on her hips '—I think we're ready.'

Stefan grabbed a tray and put some of the bowls of pasta on it. 'Patients first, then us. Let's make sure everyone is good.'

It only took a few minutes to serve the dinner and for Joe, Cathy and Lynn to be attracted by the smell and come to collect their food.

'Where do you want to eat?' asked Stefan.

All of a sudden she realised they were alone. It would be so easy to suggest they eat with some of the patients, or with their colleagues. But, for some entirely selfish reason, Paige didn't want to.

'Any place you haven't shown me yet?' There was a hint of something in her voice, and it surprised even her.

There was a flicker of recognition on Stefan's face. He smiled. 'Sure. Follow me.'

They walked down the corridor with their food, past all the rooms and around another corridor and down a few steps.

'What's this?' asked Paige, as he pushed open a door to a dark space.

He gestured for her to follow. 'Are you scared of the dark?'

'No. But why are you asking that?'

'Because if you don't mind waiting a few minutes in the dark, I might surprise you.' He leaned over and set his food down somewhere. 'Back in a sec.'

Paige had no idea how he knew where he was going. Some hidden part of her brain decided to instantly remind her of every horror movie she'd ever watched. What was that noise? Was that a shadow?

A few seconds later there was a flicker.

And then she gasped.

Dim lights came on. In front of her were a few rows of wide red velvet seats, and in front of them, on the furthest wall, was a large screen.

'A cinema!'

The screen flickered and Stefan's voice came through much louder than before. She jumped. 'Just switching things on.'

The screen came to life, and the soundtrack of a popular dinosaur movie came through the apparently hidden speakers.

Stefan appeared again through a door up a couple of steps at the back of the room.

He lifted his plate. 'Let's grab a seat. Movie's about to start.'

She shook her head. 'You have a cinema in a hospital?'

He shrugged. 'All I can say is that it's one of the most popular parts of the hospital complex in Hollywood. More popular than the gym, or the library.'

Paige still couldn't believe it. She moved along a few seats and sat down. The red velvet chair was sumptuous, deep and well-supported. Stefan sat in the one next to her, his shoulder brushing against hers.

'I can't believe this,' she said as the lights

started to dim around them, conscious that they were still touching.

'A cinema?' he asked. 'I don't think it's that unusual.'

She shot him a look as she ate a spoonful of her pasta. 'No. Not the cinema. I can't believe that a few days before Christmas you get a chance to pick a movie—I've told you about my Christmas obsession, and you still go with *Jurassic Park*.'

He grinned in the dark. 'What can I say? Who doesn't love a dinosaur?'

'If it isn't Christmas, I'm a sci-fi girl,' she grumbled good-naturedly. '*Star Trek*, *Star Wars*...'

He leaned over and whispered in her ear while laughing, his warm breath on her cheek. 'Dinosaurs are sci-fi. Get with the programme.'

There was a definite shiver down her spine. And it was nothing to do with the dark, or the dinosaurs. It was the closeness between them. The hint in the air that had been there from the moment they'd stepped down the corridor towards the cinema. Their teasing and flirtation seemed to have reached a whole different level.

Paige settled back in her chair, trying to pretend this wasn't a completely surreal experience. A private cinema. A handsome man whose warm breath had just been on her neck. And an avalanche. She couldn't make this up.

But if she could, the next part might need a rating that wasn't for dinosaur movies.

CHAPTER SIX

STEFAN LOOKED OUT of the window at the looming dark clouds. It was apparently seven a.m. He'd never seen it so dark at this time of year. It seemed that all the weather reports he'd seen were entirely accurate.

Franco had told him that the people down at the café were getting annoyed and restless. Some supplies were dwindling, and there were no proper wash facilities. Although the chalet was available, the logistics of moving people across the snow in the first instance, then up the winding road, was just too risky. Whilst it was only a five-minute drive from the edge of the resort to the chalet in Stefan's car, it would take a whole lot longer on foot.

Stefan's offer to drive down and ferry people back and forth was declined.

'Too risky,' said Franco. 'Right now, we only have people in two places. If we have another avalanche, it could hit the part near the road again. You, and your patients, are probably safer higher up and near the chalet. I wouldn't take the risk of trying to move these people, when we still can't be sure this snow won't move again. At least in here they're sheltered. Out there…' He let his voice tail off.

'Have there been any reports of anyone missing or unaccounted for?'

Franco sighed. 'Thankfully not. There were a few accounts of possible missing people, but it turned out they'd already made their way down to the village, or were up here.'

Stefan heaved a huge sigh of relief. 'Good.' He finished the call and went back to the kitchen. He'd been up for the last few hours, reluctant to start working in the main room of the suite in case he somehow disturbed Paige.

The more he got to know her, the more intrigued he was by Dr McLeod. He loved that accent. The way it got thicker as she became more passionate about a subject, or even when she became more relaxed around him.

It was hard being in close quarters with someone with that pull about them. The pull that made him want to look at her every moment and keep looking for her when she moved out of his line of sight.

Stefan was used to being around all kinds of beautiful women. Paige was naturally pretty—pale skin, good cheekbones, wide eyes and long lashes. He liked her. He liked the way her sass could bubble up and overflow. He liked the fact that she'd pulled herself together and started digging with them all after the avalanche. She was out of her comfort zone, but clearly still prepared to try her best.

But there was something about her that didn't quite sit properly. She'd talked a little about her work. She'd admitted she was here for a rest. But he couldn't help but be curious about what her story was. The bruises he'd thought he'd noticed that first day were more visible when she wore scrubs. She hadn't offered any explanation for them. And he hadn't asked. They were fading. They were recent.

Understanding Paige McLeod was like trying to put together pieces of a puzzle. But something else was bothering him.

Himself.

Stefan Bachmann didn't give himself time to think like this. Being stranded up a mountain with limited access to resources was odd. He was writing a million lists. Sending a million emails that he wasn't sure were getting through. The internet had been installed the morning of the avalanche, but it was patchy. The booster that had been dropped to them didn't seem to make much difference.

If he'd been back home, or even up here, with no avalanche, he would be *doing* things. Seeing more patients. Doing online consultations. Painting the walls if he had to.

He couldn't remember the last time he'd taken the time to sit and watch a movie. But last night, with Paige, it had just seemed to fit. It had just seemed right.

And even that made him a little uncomfortable.

Stefan had been born with a nervous energy. His mother had said she could never contain him. The school library had never had enough books. There had never been enough teams to join—football, hockey, rugby. But that energy had changed and been channelled after his mother had died. Once he'd qualified as a doctor, and finished specialising, he'd done voluntary mission after voluntary mission. And he could put his hand on his heart and say that he'd genuinely loved them. But stopping, even for a day, made his brain crowd with thoughts about treatments he should be doing, and people he should be helping. People like his mother. The one person he had failed. Working helped keep him ticking over. To push those guilty feelings from his mind and just focus on the next thing to do.

But now? Being stuck here? He was restless. He was antsy. He could have done with another ten patients or so in the hospital. Not that he wished for a second that anyone else was hurt or stranded here. But just to keep him busy.

The tracker he was using on his computer blinked. It was showing potential breaks in the weather. Trouble was, they were only lasting ten minutes at most. Not enough time to get a helicopter safely in the air and back to the hospital. He knew the journey meant the pilot and his team would be in the air for between thirty and forty minutes minimum—and there didn't look like any predicted breaks in the weather to allow that to happen.

He sighed. They were stuck up here for at least another twenty-four hours. Maybe more. Paige had told him that she loved

Christmas. She'd also mentioned how great the chalet was.

Claudia, the seven-year-old, was getting bored. Maybe he could bring some of the Christmas items from the chalet here to try and brighten the place up, make it a little more festive.

Paige had also mentioned some kind of presents. None of the adults would be worried about presents, but a seven-year-old who still believed in Santa definitely would. And it didn't matter that it might not be what she'd hoped for. There still had to be something for a little girl to open on Christmas morning.

It was time for a meeting.

He called all his new colleagues together, made coffee and sat them down in the kitchen.

'Franco called. It looks like the weather will be even worse today and an evacuation won't be possible.' Before they all had a chance to feel low, he carried on. 'I was wondering how you would all feel about trying to make this place look a bit more like Christmas.'

Frowns creased a number of foreheads and he kept speaking. 'We should be safe enough to take a few trips down to the chalet. What about the Christmas tree? And some of the other decorations? I was also thinking about Claudia.'

'Presents.' Lynn, Cathy and Paige said the word together.

They all exchanged glances. 'Is there anything there at all we can use?'

Paige wrinkled her nose. 'There should be. There are board games we can bring up. I'm sure I saw a basket with some kind of crafts. There are books. There might even be more stuff that I just didn't get a chance to find.' She held up her hands. 'I'd only arrived the night before and had a quick look around. Because of the weather, I wanted to ski the next morning, and planned to spend the next day in the chalet.' She gave a smile. 'There could be more that I didn't have time to discover.'

Stefan held up the car keys. 'When we get a break in the weather, will we take a quick trip down?'

Paige nodded and turned to the others. 'Are we worried about anyone today?'

Lynn shook her head. 'All casts are good…fingers and toes are all pink and moving. Eva has had no further concerns with her pregnancy, Bob's diabetes is fine, he's just bored. Rafe needs to be tied to the bed. I've caught him trying to get up a few times by himself and he's not quite there yet. He still needs some supervision.'

Stefan nodded, along with Paige. 'Let us know if you're worried at all again. I'll check Rafe later. Let's introduce Bob to the cinema. It might keep him entertained for a bit.'

'What cinema?' said Joe, Lynn and Cathy in unison.

Paige laughed. 'The hidden one at the end of the corridor. Stefan will show you how to use the computer and set up the films. It's a whole otherworld experience.'

Three sets of eyes widened and Cathy groaned. 'How the other half live.' It was said in jest and the rest all nodded.

When a short break in the weather was predicted, Lynn, Paige and Stefan drove down to the chalet. 'We've got to get the tree,' said Stefan as soon as they walked inside.

'Will we get that in the car?' asked Lynn.

'As long as we leave the boot open,' said Paige. She was looking around. 'Okay, Lynn, the library is along there. I didn't really get a proper chance to look, so you might find some suitable things in there.'

'Can I take anything?' she asked curiously.

Paige was hesitating and Stefan broke in. 'We can send an email and let the owner know what we've done. Here's hoping he might understand, rather than think we've just stripped his chalet clean.'

'We kind of have.' Paige pulled a face. 'I doubt there's anything left in the food cupboards. It was the best-stocked place I've seen.'

Stefan leaned back, looking around more critically. 'You know, there might never have been an avalanche here before, but maybe the owner always had that in mind. They might have had concerns about the road. Even heavy snowfall or black ice could make it unusable.'

'Is this really the best place for a hospital?'

Stefan sighed. 'It's why there's also a helipad in the plans.' He waved a hand. 'From what I remember, it's only a few times a year that the road might be dangerous.'

She leaned on the counter and put her head on her hand. 'And aren't you in charge of that now?'

He sighed. 'I'm beginning to realise exactly what that means.' He glanced over his shoulder. Lynn had gone off to the library. 'Are you unhappy that you're stuck up a mountain with me?'

'Only because you snore,' she said without a moment's hesitation.

'I do not!'

'How many times are we going to have this fight?' she asked, walking over to the large Christmas tree, trying to decide how best to move it.

There were Christmas garlands along the fireplace, and more on the stairs. 'I think we should take these too.'

Stefan looked out of the window. 'If we try and take all the decorations off the tree, it will take too long. We only have a thirty-minute window. Any ideas?'

Paige nodded and walked into the kitchen, pulling open a drawer.

Stefan smiled and, between them, they wound the clingwrap around the tree to try to keep some of the decorations in place, before tipping it on its side and wrestling it out to the car. Lynn had already loaded up some other supplies, but she had another few boxes that there just wasn't room for.

She looked at them. 'How about I take these up, and come back for the rest?'

Paige checked her watch. 'Is there enough time?'

They all looked at the sky. It was grey, but not as stormy as it had been.

For a moment, no one spoke. 'There's still a few rooms to check over,' said Paige. Her stomach was twisting a little but she nodded. 'You feel okay to drive up and back?'

Lynn nodded. 'It will take longer for the other two to help me unload at the hospital than it will to do the drive.'

Stefan pressed his lips together and put his hand on her arm. 'It looks fine now, but the weather is so changeable. All our patients are fine. If you have any concerns, or the weather gets worse, just stay.' He looked around. 'The chalet is secure and warm. We could manage.'

Lynn gave a nod. 'Don't worry, I'll be back in the blink of an eye.'

She climbed into the car and drove off. Stefan closed the door and turned back to Paige. 'Anywhere else to check?'

She nodded. 'You have no idea how big this place is. In fact, it's a bit like your hospital. A Tardis. Bigger on the inside than it looks from the outside.'

He tilted his head at her. 'A *Doctor Who* fan?'

'Wasn't every child?' Then she laughed. 'And they've started making Christmas specials. It was like someone sent them a note.'

'You didn't?' He actually looked as if he believed she might have.

She tapped the side of her nose. 'You don't get to know all my secrets because you're trapped in a chalet with me.'

Paige led him through to two more rooms near the back of the chalet. One was another sitting room with multiple cupboards, a comfortable sofa and a table and chairs. The other was smaller, with another fireplace and red squishy seats.

'This place never ends,' he said, as he headed into the room with the cupboards. A few moments later he gave a shout. 'What about this…stuff?'

She could hear the question in his voice and wandered through to see him holding a large wicker basket. It was full of wool, knitting needles and lots of little bags filled with pom-poms, sequins, beads and felt.

'Oh, wow.' Paige couldn't wipe the smile

from her face. 'This could keep Claudia happy for hours. Perfect. Good find.'

There was a loud roar of wind and they both froze.

'Oh, no…' Paige's heart started to pound. Not because she was worried for herself. 'Will Lynn have made it?'

Stefan put his hand to his pocket and let out a curse. 'The satellite phone is with Joe. Is there a phone in here that might work?'

Paige walked back out to the hallway and picked up the main phone, shaking her head when she heard no tone. 'Let me see if there's Wi-Fi. We might be able to send a message that way.'

There was an older computer in one of the rooms. She fired it up, used the password in the drawer and, after an inevitable delay, it finally connected. The internet seemed spotty. But Paige logged into her account and sent a message to Joe. Within a few minutes she got a response.

She's here. But stay where you are. Too dangerous.

Paige let out a huge sigh of relief. 'Lynn's okay. But Joe must have spoken to Franco. He says to stay.'

Stefan's expression was unreadable. He paced over to the nearest window, pressing his face so close that the glass steamed up with his breath.

'Think I'm making it up?' she quipped.

He shook his head. 'Of course not. But…' he looked around '…what will we do?'

Paige looked at him. 'Are you serious?'

'Yes.' He nodded, and it was then she realised that he was entirely serious.

'Nothing, Stefan. We'll do nothing. We'll wait. Read a book. Sit down. Watch the TV. Rummage around and hope we can find some leftover food.' She moved away from him and walked out into the corridor and along to the kitchen, running the tap. 'Look, the pipes haven't frozen or burst, so I can make you tea, coffee or hot chocolate. We can survive on that if we have to.'

He kept moving. She watched in amazement as he paced from room to room, eventually climbing the stairs. Now, she was curious. She found him in the main bedroom, looking at the mountain through the large window. He'd raised the blind she'd pulled the last time she'd been here, thinking it could protect the room a bit if the avalanche had come this way. He was looking up at the swirling grey and black clouds. It actually made her shudder.

'What are you doing? Are you hoping that a tornado will put down and sweep you off to the Emerald City?' It was easy to joke about the well-known film.

'Will there be something to do there?' he muttered.

The words stung. Was he really so worried about being alone with her? She turned and walked downstairs, taking some deep breaths. It would be so easy to be offended and take his remark personally, but Paige was wiser than that.

She knew exactly how many thoughts were swirling around her own head. Thoughts that she hadn't said out loud to anyone. Maybe Stefan was exactly the same as her.

He'd already mentioned that his dad could be alone for Christmas now. Might he be worried—or feeling guilty? She'd sent a message to her family to let them know she was safe. She'd never planned on spending Christmas with them as she'd expected to be working. She'd told them about the assault at work and that she was taking a holiday for a few weeks.

She put water in a jug and filled the coffee machine, selecting a pod with a coffee with a hint of nutmeg. She was determined to try and be a little festive. The main room was bare without the huge Christmas tree, but there were still other Christmas decorations around, and she lit the fire as the coffee gurgled through in the kitchen.

They were alone. Stranded alone in this chalet. The man whose breath on her skin the night before had sent a dozen sensations down her spine. She recognised he was feeling edgy. But she was feeling edgy too. A night alone together in this chalet might be more than she could handle. The flirtation was already there. Paige took a deep breath, trying to focus herself back on the immediate issues.

Since they were stuck here, she pulled off her boots and jacket, contemplating going upstairs for one of the luxury bathrobes. But the coffee was ready. She grabbed the mug, strolled through to the library and pulled a thriller from the shelves. A few minutes later she was curled up on the red sofa with a blanket on her knees. She could quite easily be stranded here, even if Stefan Bachmann couldn't. As for the tension between them? She would just need to see how things played out.

* * *

The swirling black clouds seemed to echo his thoughts. He'd been rude, he knew that. And he'd have to apologise.

But Stefan made his way back to the computer and sent a message to his father, hoping it would reach him. His father was quite tech savvy. He would be worried, of course he would. Even though they were sometimes thousands of miles apart, his father always knew where Stefan was.

He'd planned to spend Christmas Day and Boxing Day with his father. During the evacuation of patients to the hospital, he'd considered asking Franco for the use of the satellite telephone to get in touch. But it would have been wrong—very wrong.

He'd just made sure his name was on the list of people stuck on the mountain and trusted the people coordinating the rescue to let his father know he was safe. That would be enough for his dad. He would trust Stefan to fill in the details later, knowing that he would be staying to help as much as he could.

His head filled with pictures of his parents' house. A small settee, and two chairs around the fire—one that had been empty for twelve years.

It didn't matter where Stefan had been in the world, at Christmas time he'd always asked his father to join him. Sometimes he'd said yes, sometimes no, dependent on the potential length of the journey. But, if they couldn't be together, Stefan would video call his father at breakfast time, and at dinner time, so they could drink coffee or eat food together, sharing news and stories.

It was hard being an only child. For a time, he'd tried to persuade his father to move to Los Angeles with him, luring him with warm weather and a large, spacious home. But his father had refused. The visits were enough. The heat made his brain foggy, he complained, he preferred the fresh mountain air. Los Angeles was too spread out, he didn't want to spend his life in a car, and a variety of other excuses.

Stefan knew it was much more fundamental than that. His father would never leave the home he'd shared with his wife.

Guilt swamped him again and he drew in a deep breath. Paige didn't get it. She didn't understand that he couldn't bear to be still. He couldn't bear not to be busy. Being snowed in at a luxury chalet might be her idea of paradise, but it was his kind of trap.

A trap to keep him still. A trap to make him stop and face his demons.

He swallowed and looked out at the dark clouds. The weather would be like this for the next few hours. He'd have to contain himself. Sitting for just over two hours last night had been quiet enough. Dinosaurs and the floral scent of someone sitting next to him had at least been a part distraction.

He was aware of the sexual tension between them. He was definitely interested in Paige, and was sure she felt the same. But being stranded in a hospital with a whole host of other people was entirely different to being stranded here alone with a very sexy woman. A woman he still had to apologise to.

Stefan made his way back down the stairs. The aroma of coffee drifted towards him. He walked through to the kitchen and found the pods, hoping he was putting it in the correct way before sticking a cup underneath. Most of the cupboards had been stripped, but he found a long thin wall cabinet that contained a stash of undiscovered biscuits.

After a few seconds' contemplation, he found a plate and laid the biscuits out the way he'd seen his mother do in years gone by.

Steeling himself, he made his way through

to the room he knew Paige would be sitting in. She didn't even glance up and he knew he had to settle the tension between them.

He contemplated the single armchairs, before biting the bullet and sitting down right next to her, setting the plate of biscuits between them.

'I come in peace,' he said.

'Shoot to kill,' she replied, her face deadpan.

He choked on the coffee he'd just swallowed, coughing and spluttering.

She raised her eyebrows. 'What—you don't like the worst pop song ever about my favourite sci-fi series?'

He started to laugh, in amongst the coughing and choking. 'I can't believe I actually know what you mean. And you're right, it is the worst pop song ever.'

She gave a shrug. 'But it's moved with the times. Memes are everywhere with those words.'

He shook his head and pushed the biscuits towards her. She lifted one and frowned at him. 'Where did you find these?'

'One of the wall cupboards in the kitchen. We must have missed it before.'

'I can live on biscuits for a night,' she said, biting one in half.

He waited a second, trying not to focus on her lips, then dunked his biscuit in his coffee, letting it semi-melt before eating it quickly. He looked up to see her horror-struck expression.

'You didn't just dunk.'

'Of course I did. And don't give me that. I've worked in Scotland. Everyone in Scotland dunks.'

'Everyone in Scotland does *not* dunk. *I* do not dunk,' Paige said indignantly. He liked her when she had that glint in her eye.

'You don't know what you're missing,' he whispered as he stuck his biscuit back into his coffee.

'It's tea you dunk with, not coffee. No one dunks in coffee,' she protested.

Stefan raised his eyebrows and lifted his biscuit back out of his coffee. Then, as if in slow motion, the weight of the coffee-laden biscuit made it waver, then split in the middle, break and land in the coffee with a *thunk*.

Paige was done for. She dissolved into fits of laughter. She had to put her own cup onto the table at the side of the sofa before she rolled onto the floor.

Stefan was sitting frozen, paralysed at the catastrophe that had been his coffee and biscuit. He peered into the cup and shook his head as he glanced at Paige. 'There's no hope, is there?'

She was on her back on the floor at this point. 'Nope—' she laughed '—none at all.'

Stefan reached down and pulled her up by the hand, landing her halfway onto his lap. 'I'm glad I've managed to amuse you,' he said wryly, liking their close proximity.

But she knew he was joking. He wondered if she might pull away. But she didn't.

Instead, she sort of snuggled into him, leaving them both on the sofa together. She didn't say much—as if she didn't want to draw much attention to their now ultra-close positioning. Instead she grabbed the TV remote. 'Today, I get to choose.'

She flicked through the channels, her warm body heating him. Stefan had no wish to move at all.

'Well, looks like you get your wish, just about everything is Christmas,' he murmured in her ear. He could feel the heat of her body close to his.

She settled on an old Christmas movie. 'Perfect.'

'Perfect,' he echoed. He'd probably seen it a dozen times in his life, but it was one of those Christmas films that no one minded—

harmless and entertaining—plus his mind was currently on other things. He definitely needed the distraction.

All of a sudden he wasn't thinking about all the work things he could be doing. He wasn't thinking about referrals, surgeries, or even how many renovations the hospital still needed and estimating the exact opening date.

No. Stefan Bachmann was thinking about something else. Someone else.

Paige leaned back a little, her hair brushing against his nose. She really was comfortable. He moved his arm slightly, settling his hand on her hip. He couldn't pretend he wasn't interested in this Scottish doctor. The girl who loved Christmas but had come up here to escape. Who'd somehow found herself in a baron's hideaway luxury chalet, that was available for people like her.

As the light seemed to fade from outside, warm, dim lights automatically switched on inside the room. The peach glow bathed the side of Paige's face, and he noticed an old wound. It was mainly healed, but it was still red and angry, as if the crust had just fallen off.

He stiffened, automatically worrying about her, all his senses moving into protective mode. Should he really ask questions if he wasn't prepared for the answers?

But Stefan was a doctor. Of course he would. In a soft voice he spoke next to her ear. 'What happened to your head? Were you skiing before? Did you fall?'

He felt her stiffen against him too, but only for a few seconds before she slumped back against him. 'No. That was work. A&E. A drunken patient slammed me into a wall.'

He felt instant rage. The fury at someone attacking a fellow worker. He sat up a little. 'What happened? Wasn't there anyone there to help?'

She sighed and shook her head. 'If you've worked in A&E you know how these things happen in the blink of an eye. You don't have time to think about anything. It's just a minor head wound. The bruises on my back are worse.'

'But it shouldn't happen,' he said angrily.

She turned her head sideways to glance at him. 'We don't all work in the Hollywood Hills, Stefan. I work in the roughest part of Glasgow and see all sorts. Some of the people are the salt of the earth, and would give you the shoes off their feet, others are victims of alcohol, drugs or domestic abuse. It takes all sorts.' He thought she was going to stop, and for some reason he could tell that she normally would have, but instead she took a big breath. 'I've been kind of unlucky. It's the third time I've been assaulted in six months. The second time was actually the worst—I had to go for a head CT. That's why I'm here. After it happened again my boss sent me away for a few weeks. He knew about this place and arranged it for me. They're making changes at A&E, bringing in more staff, and some security. It should all be in place when I get back. I think he feels guilty.'

'He should. You never should have been assaulted once, never mind three times. That's ridiculous, for any hospital, I don't care where it is.'

For a second, he thought he saw her blink back tears, and he was ready for her to come out fighting. But instead she leaned back against him again. 'I'm just tired,' she said quietly. 'Tired of it all.'

Something struck a nerve in him and he tried to understand why he suddenly felt so protective of her.

He placed his hand over hers, squeezing it gently, then stroking the back of her hand. 'I know this hasn't exactly been the time away you wanted, but, if there are changes, things might be better when you go back.'

Actually, he didn't want to say that at all. He wanted to tell her to leave her job and come to Los Angeles. He could talk to friends. Find her a job somewhere half decent. Somewhere you didn't need a bodyguard to keep you safe at work.

There was a long silence. Her voice was shaky. 'What if I don't want to go back?'

Now, he sat up fully and pushed her up too, just so he could adjust his position and they were facing each other. 'Paige, what are you saying?'

A tear slid down her face. 'Do you ever feel like not being a doctor any more? Do you ever think you should find something else to do?'

It was like a punch to the guts. He planned to spend his whole life helping people. He owed that to his mum and dad. He would never, ever consider walking away. How could anyone do that, when they had the passion for the job that he had?

He could see how upset she was, so he answered carefully. 'No, I've never felt like that. And I can't imagine ever feeling like that. Being a doctor was all I ever wanted to do. My mum and dad made a lot of sacrifices to let me go to medical school. I don't have enough hours in the day. I'm always planning my next consultation, or surgery, or trip for Médecins Sans Frontières.' He put his hand to his chest. He wanted to say these words with fervour and passion, because that was how he honestly felt. But he knew he had to tread gently. He wasn't a clown.

'Don't you still feel the passion inside? The buzz when you wake up in the morning? The feeling that, no matter what, you will be doing some good?'

More tears spilled down her cheeks. She shook her head. 'Honestly? No, I don't. I haven't for the last few months.' She put both hands up to her face and covered her eyes. 'I'm the worst doctor in the world. My heart isn't in it any more. When the avalanche hit, I panicked. When you pulled me to the floor, all I could remember was the assaults. I had to come and help, of course I would do that. But up at the hospital, when you asked me if I wanted to leave?' She swallowed and pulled her hands away from her face. 'For the smallest possible second, I actually thought about it. Who does that, Stefan? Who actually does that?'

His blood felt chilled. This was the total

opposite to how he felt about things. How he wanted his life to be. But he could see the pain written all over her face. He lifted his hand to her cheek. 'Maybe your boss was right. Maybe you just need some time away and some space to get your head clear. You did help, Paige. You helped in an emergency situation. And you helped in surgery—something you never usually do. You stepped up. You did that. And you did a good job.'

She nodded slowly, her dark eyes fixed on his. 'But what about later?' Her voice was shaking.

He pulled her into a hug. 'Don't think about later. Not right now. You've just been involved in an avalanche. You're essentially cut off from the world. This isn't the time or place to make life-changing decisions. Don't think about any of this.'

A tune started playing on the TV on the wall behind them, reminding him of the Christmas movie. He wrapped one arm around her shoulder. 'Here, think about Christmas. Think about celebrating. Because if we're still stuck here, that's what we'll do.'

He could sense the tiny tremor in her. He guessed she'd never had this conversation with someone before. And he wasn't sure he was the best person to assist, when he felt so strongly and passionately about his job.

It didn't help that he was currently fighting such feelings of attraction towards her. Paige was beautiful. He'd seen her working...he'd seen her spark. He honestly believed that back home she would be a wonderful doctor. She'd studied hard for years. It had just been an unlucky few months. He should distract her. Let her think about something else for a while.

He wanted to keep talking. But, deep down, something stopped him. He might hear something he didn't like. She might question his passion and his motives. She might uncover his guilt. Things that he didn't need right now.

He looked around. The chalet was warm, beautiful and comfortable. They were safe here. And for some reason that was the thing that struck hardest. Because, above all else, he wanted to make Paige McLeod feel safe.

The Christmas movie danced across the screen. It really was one of her favourites. The flickering fire, the reds and greens of the decorations that were left, and the cosy feel of Stefan's arm around her shoulder, and his warm body next to hers was something she would never even have imagined a few days ago.

But here she was, having just poured her heart out to another doctor, and admitted she might not still want to be one.

She could tell he was surprised, and shocked. Just like everyone else might be if she told them too. But telling someone she'd only spent a few days with seemed like a good testing ground.

He'd been nice, and she got the feeling he might have been holding back. When he'd fixed those blue eyes on hers it had seemed all right to tell the truth, to try and loosen the heavy weight on her shoulders. Maybe he'd brushed off what she'd said a little, but at least he'd allowed her to talk, to have that conversation, and he hadn't shouted or been angry with her. He hadn't told her she was stupid. He'd told her to take some time, think about something else for a while.

And she was. Stefan Bachmann.

The heat of his body was doing strange things to her. She'd thought he was attractive the first moment she'd met him on the road and he'd raged at her driver. When he'd approached her in the ski café for 'stealing' his chair, she'd enjoyed the gentle flirtation and teasing. It had been fun. And it was a long time since Paige had experienced fun.

As for all the rest? The way her eyes had boggled out of her head when he'd stepped out of the shower, his dedication to his job, and the few surprises she'd found here and there. It all added up to someone she wanted to know more about, and a guy she was immensely attracted to.

Being snowed in, in a chalet in the mountains, had its plus points.

'What would be your ideal dream date?' she asked, her head lying against his shoulder and her eyes now closed.

'Where did that come from?' She could hear the amused tone in his voice.

'Let's call it a cosy enquiry?'

'You're feeling cosy?'

'Who wouldn't?'

He was quiet for a few moments and she nearly opened her eyes, but then he started speaking. 'Dream date is a strange question. I haven't done much dating in a while.'

'Don't tell me.' She was smiling, 'No time.'

'How did you know that?'

Now she did open her eyes and look at him. 'Let's just say, in the few days I've known you, I've kind of got that impression.'

She patted her hand on his chest since it was so close. 'So, no secret wife or fiancée in five countries, or a million dating apps and a hundred conversations going on at once.'

He laughed. He actually laughed. 'I can't keep up with one dating app, and one conversation, let alone multiples.' He shook his head. 'Plus, it's hard. I'm going between Los Angeles and Switzerland. I'm doing the jobs for Médecins Sans Frontières and they can take me anywhere. And…' he shrugged '… I do occasionally like to ski.'

She sat up and smiled. 'So you *do* actually take holidays?'

'Occasionally. In fact, that would be my dream date. A day on an off-piste ski run.'

'Seriously?'

'What?'

She let her head flop back. 'I give up. I ask about the dream date, and I get a ski run. Thick, fumbly clothes, skis and poles, danger, speed, and what part of skiing involves touching?' she asked indignantly.

'Ah… So that's what you were looking for.' He was teasing now. 'You wanted dinner in an exclusive restaurant, or on a beach somewhere, with sexy clothes or swimsuits. A private castle. A Learjet.'

Their eyes locked. 'Can't a girl have the simple things in life?'

He moved closer, his nose just a few inches from hers. She could feel his warm breath on her skin and see the shadow around his chin line.

'So, whereabouts did the touching come into this dream date?'

She raised her eyebrows. 'Now, that's a loaded question.'

'Or a lucky one. Do you think being snowed in, in a luxury chalet, will count?' He glanced down. 'We forgot the black suit, bow tie and evening dress.'

She nodded in agreement. 'Formal dress clothes, I've always found them quite restrictive.'

'Me too.' He moved his hand. It was almost back to its former position at her waist, but this time her shirt and jeans had separated a little and his fingers brushed her skin. Paige didn't object. Not for a second.

She put her hand on his shoulder. 'I guess I can make an exception for one day.'

'If we can get to the touching?'

She ran her finger along his jaw line. 'If we can get to the touching,' she repeated.

He moved then, leaning forward and connecting his lips with hers. There was a hint of coffee, but all she could really focus on was the sensations sweeping over every part of her. The kiss deepened, their bodies moving even closer, moulding into each other.

She ran her hands through his dark hair, then bringing them back around to his face, letting his stubble rub against her palms. Heat was rising inside her. Clothes which had felt cosy were now uncomfortably warm.

He shifted his weight and she moved automatically, leaning back into the sofa. His blue eyes fixed on hers. 'Is this okay?' There it was. His accent. Thicker than ever. Sexier than ever. She might have to change her idea of a dream date.

'Yes,' she said with certainty, and his lips started to move over her face and down her neck. In turn her hands slid down his sides, feeling his defined muscles and muscle tone.

Nothing had felt this good. Nothing had lit the fire inside her quite like this. So, for now, Paige McLeod didn't waste a second thinking about anything else.

CHAPTER SEVEN

IT WAS A strange sensation—waking up wrapped in the arms of someone who, a few days ago, had been a perfect stranger.

But Paige wasn't worried. This was an extraordinary situation. Maybe some time when she was an old woman she'd tell her grandchildren about the avalanche and being snowed in on a mountain in the Swiss Alps.

Would she tell them everything? Who could tell?

It was morning. She knew that automatically, but someone had forgotten to tell the weather. It was still pitch-black outside. At this time a few days ago the sun had been clearly visible and people were already heading to the ski runs to hit the first snow.

Today, skiing was out of the question. From the look of it, evacuation might be out of the question too.

She gave Stefan a nudge. 'Christmas Eve,

and it looks like we're going to have to play Santa.'

He wrinkled his nose, clearly not quite awake yet. 'What?'

His eyes flickered open and he looked at the window nearest them, which was showing no signs of daylight. Recognition flared in his eyes and he sat up. 'Oh, yeah. Darn it.'

He looked back at her, as if wondering how to be after a night entwined together. 'Okay?'

She smiled. 'Okay, but you're making breakfast—partly because you managed to find some spare food last night.'

He stretched and nodded. 'I'll take the challenge. Why don't you see if there's anything on the news?'

She waited until he left, then climbed up to the bathroom she'd been using. She'd left a few things behind, so jumped in the shower, changed into the last remaining clothes she had, and washed and dried her hair and brushed her teeth. Paige always carried two toothbrushes—a habit she'd got into as a junior doctor, and she'd never grown out of.

By the time she got back down the stairs an aroma was wafting towards her. As she walked into the kitchen it was clear Stefan had mastered the coffee machine. He gestured her to take a seat at the kitchen island.

'What's in there?' She pointed to the oven.

'I found some croissants in the freezer. Unfortunately, we've taken all the butter up to the hospital, so it's marmalade or raspberry jam.'

'Jam,' she said decisively. 'Remind me to let you make breakfast again. I hadn't even found the freezer.'

The oven timer pinged and Stefan slid the croissants out onto a plate, which he put between them. 'Delicious,' breathed Paige. They were hot and crisp on the outside, but fluffy on the inside and perfect with the jam, and the coffee.

'Did you hear anything on the news?'

She shook her head. 'I went up into the shower. I turned it on but didn't really get a chance to listen. It's still so dark. Do you really think there'll be a break in the weather?'

He heaved a big sigh. 'We've got to hope there's at least one where we can get back up to the hospital. I know the likelihood is that everyone is fine, but I'd still feel better if we could check.'

We. He'd used the 'we' word. She wasn't sure if he'd used it before. But this time she'd noticed. It seemed kind of nice.

'We have Christmas presents to take for a little girl,' she reminded him.

'Little girls aren't my speciality, but since we have a whole host of adult females at the hospital I'm hoping for great things.'

The name of the ski resort drifted through from the television in the next room and they both turned their heads in unison and hurried through.

The sight that met them was not pleasant. The TV crew were clearly at the other side of the blocked road. There were yellow and orange road vehicles and equipment all behind the immense pile of snow, trees and debris. If they'd made any kind of indent in it, it wasn't noticeable. The TV presenter was talking rapidly in German, and Paige could catch the odd word. But the message was clear. It would take days to safely clear the road.

The presenter started gesturing with his arms skyward and holding up his hands. It looked as if helicopter rescue might be off the cards too. 'Do you think the rest of the people will have enough food?' Paige asked.

Stefan nodded. 'They've dropped essentials to them too. Food, some clothing, and medicines. Everyone at the café is fine and apparently in good spirits—just all anxious to get home.'

Paige let out a slow breath. At least there was nothing too much to worry about. 'We'll be fine,' she said with a smile.

He leaned his head on one hand. 'The only thing I actually miss is the Christmas cookies.'

She frowned. 'What do you mean?'

'Christmas cookies. They're normally everywhere. Usually start pre-Advent. There's so many different kinds I couldn't even tell you.'

She sat down next to him and mimicked his pose. 'But this is Christmas trivia, and I love it. Tell me your two favourite kinds of Christmas cookie.'

'Oh, that's easy.' His face broke into a huge smile. *Spitzbuben* are jam-filled sandwich cookies and usually have a hint of vanilla, and *Basler brunsli* are chocolate and hazelnut, sometimes with a hint of cinnamon. And *Zimtsterne* are cinnamon stars. My mother made the best in the world of all three.'

His face fell. As if the memory had just slayed him.

The words registered with her instantly. Past tense. She gave his hand a squeeze. 'We might have the ingredients to make some. We took some up to the hospital, and I'm sure there are some other things still in the store here.' Something else struck her. 'What do you have for Christmas dinner in Switzerland? Will we be able to match it?'

The spark had gone from his eyes. He spoke quietly. '*Filet em tieg* and *shinkli em tieg*, usually with potato salad, and sometimes a meat fondue.'

Paige tilted her head to one side. She loved hearing about Christmas traditions. 'What are the first two things?'

He gave a wry smile. 'We like pastry in Switzerland. The first is pork fillet with sausage meat wrapped in pastry, the second is hot ham wrapped in pastry. I'm not sure if we'll have anything like that up at the hospital.'

'There were definitely cans of new potatoes. We could make potato salad out of them. And what about the freezer I never found? Was there anything else in there? Pork fillets or ham or...' she took a breath and licked her lips '...turkey?'

A smile flickered across his lips. 'You want the whole shebang, don't you? The huge turkey with stuffing and gravy—a traditional British Christmas?'

'Truthfully, I'll take whatever we've got, or anything we can magic into something kind of special. Everyone up there will want to be at home. We need to try and make things special, even if it's only for a few hours.'

He nodded and stood up, wrapping his arm around her shoulders and kissing her on the side of the head. 'Let's do a final raid of this place. As soon as there's a break in the weather, one of the others will likely drive down for us and we can make it back up there.'

It should have been a tense few hours, watching out of the window while checking for messages and drinking even more coffee. But Paige was relaxed around Stefan. Well, as relaxed as a girl could be when it felt as if the human being next to her oozed sex appeal from every pore.

There had been more kissing, more private moments. The news had continued its reporting on the avalanche. There had been no deaths, but a few people had been seriously injured further down the valley and a number of properties and roads had been destroyed.

'Are you going to get an enormous bill for all this?'

Stefan shuddered. 'I'm trying not to think about it. When we signed the contract for the hospital, we agreed to take over upkeep and maintenance of the road. I'm sure there were some clauses, but since I'm not a lawyer I don't pay attention to those kinds of details.'

'Oops...' She smiled. 'That could be expensive.'

He nodded. 'I'm sure that if there is some kind of natural disaster—' he waved his hand '—like an avalanche, then the government take some of the responsibility for emergency aid. I'm hoping it might cover clearing the road. After that? I'm assuming my company will have to pay for some repairs. The road was in reasonable condition, but wasn't great. It might be easier to try and resurface it once the weather is better, rather than wait too much longer.'

'Was the road always like this? You said your great-grandparents met up at the hospital. Did you ever visit with your mum and dad?'

For a moment she wondered if it was the wrong question. There was a hint of something on his face. Then he gave her a resigned look. 'I only came up here once or twice, and because I was so young I never really thought about the road. It's always been like this though—narrow and windy.'

Paige licked her lips. She knew from his previous words that his mother must be dead. She didn't really want to push, but it felt reasonable to ask him a little more. 'Tell me about your parents. Did they always live here? What did they do?'

His blue eyes met hers. His look was cautious, and sincere. 'They went to school together. Grew up in the same village. My father still lives there. I don't think he'll ever move, even though I've invited him out to Los Angeles. He was a printer in a local company. When printing wasn't digital, and much more manual. He dealt with the mechanics of the machinery.' There was a long pause. 'My mum only started working when I went to school. She worked full-time after I told them I wanted to go to medical school.' He gave a sad kind of smile. 'It was expensive for two working class parents. But they were delighted I wanted to go to medical school, and probably relieved I was clever enough.'

'They must have been very proud when you qualified as a doctor,' Paige said.

A wave of sadness crossed over him. It was so clear. 'She never really got to see that part. I was just about to finish medical school when she died.' He shook his head. 'My father phoned to say she was sick, and by the time I got there...' His voice tailed off and she noticed his fists were clenched.

'You couldn't have known.' She touched the side of his arm.

His voice was sharp. 'But maybe I could have, if I'd asked the right questions. Apparently she'd been sick for a while. She'd had symptoms but hadn't had time to see a doctor. I'd only been earning a salary for a few months at this point, and my parents were still helping clear some debts from all the training and living away from home. She was working harder than she should have been. She should have been spending the money on herself, and her care, rather than still supporting her adult son.'

Paige rubbed her hand up his arm. 'But that's the way it is in lots of countries, for lots of trainees. Most people I know come out of medical school loaded with debt.'

There was a flash of anger in his eyes,

and she was wise enough to know it wasn't aimed at her. It was aimed at himself. She'd been feeling guilty about considering not being a doctor any more. But Stefan's guilt was even more ingrained—and much more damaging than contemplating a career change.

It was as if a veil came over him, some kind of spell that changed the expression on his face, and his mind-set. 'Tell me about your parents,' he said.

He wanted to change the subject. Maybe he felt he'd revealed too much. Paige wouldn't press any further. 'They're both still in Scotland. They split up a few years ago, and I'm an only child, so it makes things a little awkward. My mum met someone else and remarried. My dad also met someone else, but she died a few years after they met, so he's on his own right now.'

'Do you see them?'

She nodded. 'I do.' She wiggled her hand. 'There's still a bit of animosity, but mostly they are over things. My dad moved to the east coast, so he lives in Portobello near Edinburgh. It's a beautiful town, right on the Firth of Forth. My mum lives in Helensburgh. It's on the water too.'

Stefan wrinkled his nose at her expression and she laughed.

'"On the water" means by the coast or by a river or loch.'

'Ah, I get it. You're lucky. Lots of Scotland is on the water.'

A little alarm sounded on her phone and she pulled it from her pocket, holding it up as soon as she saw the message. 'Look! This might be it.'

She ran over to the window and stared outwards, and upwards. 'What do you think?'

He moved next to her. 'I never even got to see what that was. I'm assuming it's a potential break in the weather?'

She nodded. 'It does look a little better. Still windy. But not quite as grey. Do you think they will come for us?'

Stefan spent a few moments staring outside then smiled in agreement. 'The rest of today will be horrendous. If there's a chance to get out it's now. Let's be ready.'

The two of them spent the next five minutes rushing around, pulling on their jackets, washing cups and ensuring the chalet was tidy, pulling blinds again and checking door locks. By the time they were ready, Paige had managed to bring along another few carrier bags.

As if by magic, Joe pulled up in the car, looking relieved they were ready to go. He gestured with his hand for them to hurry. They climbed in with their packages.

'Everyone okay?' was Stefan's first question.

Joe nodded. 'We will be, once we get you two back to the hospital.'

Snow had fallen again last night but the large tyres and thick tread managed well. Paige was glad that Joe drove slowly, conscious there could be debris blown onto the road by the raging winds of the last day and night. But, apart from a few branches, it wasn't too bad.

Rain and snow started to fall again, and by the time the hospital came into sight it was pure relief. The lights were on, and the stained-glass windows were almost like warm Christmas tree lights, welcoming them home. Joe jumped out as soon as they pulled up at the doors.

Paige reached over and squeezed Stefan's hand. 'Thank you,' she breathed.

'What for?'

'For being you.' She gave him a grateful smile. 'Last night and today weren't half as scary as they could have been. Maybe no one has told you for a while, but you're good company.'

She bent over and kissed his cheek. 'Now, let's get back in and see how our kids are,' she joked.

Stefan was carrying the bags inside as Joe shook his head. 'No helicopter for us today. Winds are just too high. They did mention there might be some possibility tomorrow.'

'On Christmas Day?'

Joe nodded, watching as Lynn and Paige seemed to be whispering together, looking inside some of the new bags. 'Conspiring already. What on earth have you brought back?'

Stefan sighed. 'It looks like we might all become Father Christmas tonight. Paige and I found lots of craft things. We might be able to pull together some small things for Claudia.' He looked at Joe. 'Anything I need to worry about?'

'Absolutely not. Most patients are just a bit fed up. But we're safe, warm and comfortable.'

Stefan nodded. 'Well, I found a freezer in the chalet, and we should be able to bring together something decent for Christmas dinner.'

As they walked down the corridor, he stopped dead. The room to his left was a communal sitting room, and Joe and the others had set up the Christmas tree from the chalet, along with the lights. It looked spectacular. Claudia and her mother were sitting on a sofa watching TV. Eva, Frances and Bob were playing cards at a table. Greta had her foot up on a small stool and was reading a book.

He couldn't help but smile. 'How is everyone?' he asked, walking into the room.

Several of the guests let out a cheer. 'You're back. Are you both okay?'

He nodded and made his way around the room, asking everyone in turn if they had any problems, or needed anything. Bob had a twinkle in his eye. 'What have you done with Paige? Where is our good lady doc?'

'She came back with some more food. I think she's gone along to the kitchen.'

But Bob wasn't finished. 'Must have been a long, long night in that old chalet. Did you have to cuddle up to keep warm?'

Claudia's mother, Marie, looked up and laughed. 'Stop it, Bob. You'll embarrass him.'

Bob held out his hands. 'What, a handsome doc holed up with a gorgeous Scottish girl—everyone likes a good romance,' he said, nodding his head at Greta's book.

Everyone was listening now. All eyes were on Stefan. He didn't mind some good humour, but definitely didn't want to start any rumours. 'Paige and I got on fine. The chalet is like here, warm, comfortable, and I found an undiscovered cupboard full of biscuits. It was a win-win situation.'

He could tell from Bob's suspicious but gleeful glance that he'd been hoping for a whole lot more information, but that was all Stefan was prepared to say.

'Dr Stefan?' The small voice came from Claudia, who had her leg propped up on the sofa.

He moved over and bent down next to her. 'What is it, Claudia?'

'Can you take me home now? I wrote my letter to Santa and he won't know where to find me if I don't get home today.' Her voice was a bit wobbly and her mum shot Stefan a helpless look.

He put his hand out to Claudia. 'Don't worry, Claudia. If you can't get home, Santa always knows where every boy and girl is. I'm sure he'll leave you some presents here, and some others at home. He'll find you.'

'I won't get to see Daddy?'

There was a definite lump in Stefan's throat. He might not have children, but that didn't mean he couldn't empathise or understand how this little girl might be feeling, and how strong her mum was having to be.

'You will get to see Daddy. I promise. But we have to be sure that the road is cleared and is safe to go down, or the winds have stopped and the helicopter can fly safely. We might be here another few days, but you will definitely get to see your daddy again, and you will definitely get to open the presents that Santa leaves at home for you, as well as the ones you get here.'

Claudia's face was still sad, but she looked marginally placated. Stefan gave her another smile. 'It will all be fine. Just wait and see.'

He walked back along the corridor and found Cathy, Lynn and Paige in the kitchen. It was clear they were still plotting. Ingredients were everywhere, along with all the craft materials. 'How is your sewing?' asked Paige.

He tipped his head to the side. 'Really?'

Lynn started laughing. 'Hey, you might be able to stitch skin, but can you sew felt and sequins? We need a stocking to fill with Santa's presents.'

Stefan walked over to the selection of

items on the counter. 'I think I can rise to the challenge.'

Cathy turned to the others. 'So, I'll take some of these things along to Claudia and Marie and ask if they want to make some decorations for the tree.'

'Fabulous idea,' agreed Paige. 'That should keep her occupied for a while.'

Joe walked in with a piece of paper in his hand. 'Which Christmas movie are we watching tonight? I found *White Christmas*, *The Santa Clause*, *Santa Claus: The Movie* and *The Christmas Chronicles*.'

'All of them,' said Paige immediately.

'There's no way I can stay awake that long,' joked Cathy.

'Can we take a vote?' said Lynn. 'Watching a Christmas movie in that cinema will be perfect for Christmas Eve. I wonder if we can make popcorn and hot chocolate?'

Stefan shifted on his feet slightly awkwardly. 'What if I said I hadn't actually seen any of them?'

Four faces turned around in horror.

'What?'

'No way.'

'You're joking?'

But Paige just raised her eyebrows. 'Well,

that's perfect. That just means you have to sit up with me and watch them all.'

Stefan was conscious of all eyes on him. He gave a good-natured shrug. 'If that's my punishment I can take it. Just remember though, I'm in charge of dinner tomorrow. It could be late.'

'Oh, no,' said Joe with a broad grin on his face. 'Because, before we start the movie marathon, I'll help you prepare everything you need for tomorrow. All you have to do is slide things in the oven, or put them on the stove.'

Paige's eyes were shining. And Stefan was struck by how good-spirited everyone was being. Like him, they all had other places to be, and would miss Christmas with their family or friends, but none of these guys had complained. Hardly any of the patients had complained either, just looked a little wistful. Yet here they all were, offering to help, pull things together and make the best of their situation. He really couldn't ask for any more.

Paige pulled her hair up into a ponytail and unpacked one of the aprons she'd brought from the chalet, moving over to scrub her hands at the sink. She was always thinking of others, always pulling her weight. He could tell from the expression on her face, and in her eyes, that she was happy right now—comfortable. And that made him think that maybe he could ask for more.

The thought stilled him. His previous relationships had always been fleeting. He'd been too busy with work to pay proper attention to any of the women he'd dated. Things had always ended on good terms, with him generally being told he didn't have time for a woman in his life. But none of his previous dates had the same effect on his heart that Paige was currently having. None of them had made him want to sit down and think about someone else properly.

Maybe this was a false situation. They were snowed in, with limited contact with the outside world. It was the first time in for ever he'd actually been forced to slow down and think.

But thinking brought regrets. The same ones that were on constant repeat. If he'd asked his mother questions. If he'd come home a few days earlier. If he'd taken the time to ask how she was doing, how her health was, how she was feeling. But what young adult actually did that? His head had been in so many other places.

Stefan's mother had died because he was

selfish. Too absorbed in the world of learning and medicine to actually use his skills where they would have been most useful.

'Hey.' He jolted at the tug on his sweater. Paige was looking at him with those big dark eyes of hers. 'You okay? You looked like you were in another place.' Her voice was quiet and discreet.

He blinked. 'Yes, I'm fine. Just a bit distracted.'

He could see Joe was staring at the food that had been stashed in the hospital freezer. 'I'd better go and sort things out with Joe, I'll see you in the cinema later?'

She gave him a smile. 'It's a date.'

Paige wasn't quite sure what she was doing with her life. All she knew was that, even though she was in a strange place, and had participated in emergency medical care, she felt better than she had in a long time. And part of the reason for that was Stefan Bachmann.

She couldn't explain it. Couldn't give a real rationale for why she was feeling like this. Were there fireworks? Yes. Was there sizzle? Absolutely. But there was something else.

He was like a warm comfort blanket

around her. Someone she could talk to. Someone she could tell the things she hadn't been saying out loud. Then there had been their connection last night…

Cathy and Lynn were sorting out ingredients over on the counter top. She went over and joined them. 'I was thinking, since we are in Switzerland, we could try and make some of their Christmas cookies.'

Both women looked at her in surprise and nodded. 'What a good idea. Do you know what we need?'

She frowned and thought hard. 'Stefan told me the name of the ones his mother used to make. We could look them up and see if we have the ingredients?'

Five minutes later, after a quick search on the computer in the office, Cathy, Lynn and Paige had three separate recipes. All three donned aprons and laid out their ingredients, switching the oven on.

Lynn smiled. 'I should probably warn you that Joe is much better at cooking and baking than me. But, since he's helping with the dinner for tomorrow, we should just leave him to it.' She waggled her hand. 'My attempts can be a bit hit or miss.'

Cathy laughed. 'Well, we're all making

something for the first time. If it's a disaster, I can make cupcakes.'

'Deal,' agreed Paige. She pulled out a large pan and set it on the stove. 'And let's not forget the popcorn either. I feel like I'm in my favourite TV baking show. And there is absolutely no way I'd ever win that.'

'Same,' agreed Cathy. 'Didn't a doctor win it once?'

'Well, it certainly wasn't me, but I'll have a bash,' said Paige.

She'd never been in a situation like this before. The most she'd made with friends had been stir fry or beans on toast. Any baking had been very much a solo effort, so it was nice to be amongst colleagues.

As she started measuring out ingredients, she could feel eyes on her. She looked up. Stefan was moving some things from the freezer and into the fridge. Others, he covered over and set out on one of the worktops, obviously to defrost for tomorrow. They might be in an unexpected predicament, but the truth was they were extremely lucky.

A little frisson darted down her spine. This guy was beyond handsome. The crinkles around his blue eyes, his dark hair and tall, lean frame made her mind go to a million places it probably shouldn't. The edges of his lips turned upwards, and for a moment she suspected his mind was in exactly the same place as hers.

At that moment Paige heard the satellite phone sound and she turned to pick it up, hearing Franco's familiar voice. It brought her back to earth with a bump. 'Ah, you got back safely. Are you both okay?'

'Of course. How is everyone with you?'

'Tired. Bored. One man is fractious. Causing trouble and threatening to make his own way down the mountain.'

Paige was shocked at someone being, quite frankly, so stupid. 'What will you do?'

'Well, I can't lock him up, even if I want to. It's dangerous out there. I've been warned there could be another avalanche.'

'Really? No! What should we do?'

'Stay put. The snowfall has been heavy these past few days. They don't think it would be anything like as bad as the first. But temperatures have been fluctuating, so they've given us a warning. Above all, stay put. You will be fine where you are.'

'But will you all? Will you be in the path of another avalanche?'

Around her, four heads shot around at her words.

'No,' said Franco. 'At least we shouldn't be. But they do think the road could be affected. As soon as the weather calms, it looks like they will get us all out by helicopter.'

Paige swallowed and breathed slowly. She'd never been in a helicopter before, and wasn't really looking forward to it. But if that was the only way down the mountain in the near future, so be it.

She ended the call and shared the news.

All faces went serious. There was nothing any of them could do. 'Do we tell the others?' she asked.

'Later,' said Stefan. 'We have no right to keep it from them. But let them all enjoy the movies first.' He moved over, closer to the ladies. 'What are you all up to?'

Cathy answered first. 'Never you mind. Just go and take care of dinner for tomorrow. We'll give you a shout shortly. And remember, you've got sewing to do later.'

He gave a nonchalant wave. 'Don't worry. It will be the best Christmas stocking you've ever seen.'

'Promises, promises,' teased Paige with a twinkle in her eye.

Forty minutes later, the smell of baked cookies, popcorn and hot chocolate filled the room. They piled everything onto trays and made their way down to the cinema, where the doors were jammed open and *Santa Claus: The Movie* was poised to start. All the others—except Rafe, who'd declined to come along—were poised in their seats.

'What's that?' asked Claudia as she saw the trays.

'We have cookies,' Paige said with a smile as she slid the tray onto a table that Bob had set up. Stefan moved next to her and stopped dead. Lynn and Cathy were busy handing out the hot chocolate, so hadn't noticed his reaction.

Paige slid her arm around his waist. 'I paid attention,' she said quietly. 'You told me these were your favourites, and we've attempted to make them, to bring a little bit of Switzerland to the Christmas we have up here.' He was standing very still, staring at the plates of cookies. 'I'm sure they won't taste anywhere near as good as your mum's. But I thought it might be a nice way to remember her.'

He looked at her, his blue eyes moist. 'How did you even remember?'

She smiled at him. 'I know you distracted me with other things, but it seemed important. I told Lynn and Cathy you'd mentioned cookies being a tradition, and which ones you liked. They were delighted to give it a go.' She moved her arm and nudged him. 'Here,' she handed him a small plate. 'Take some and give them a try.'

She noticed the slight tremble to his hand as he picked up one of each of the three kinds of cookie. *Zimtsterne*, *Spitzbuben* and *Basler brunsli* had been recreated to the best of their abilities. Paige picked up a hot chocolate for him and added marshmallows and cream, beckoning him to join her in one of the large comfortable cinema seats. He sank down next to her and stared at his plate.

'Go on then,' she encouraged. It only took him a few minutes to finish them all. The cookies were small, only a few bites each. 'What's your favourite?' she asked.

'Which ones did you make?' he asked carefully.

She waved her finger at him. 'Oh, no. You don't get to trick me into revealing which are mine.' She straightened in her chair. 'Come on, give us the old *Bake-Off* twinkly eyes criticism,' she said, referring to the chef linked with the TV programme.

'I'm not quite that old,' he said indignantly.

'But you do have twinkly eyes.' She smiled back as he contemplated her question.

He sighed. 'Okay, favourite is always any cookie with jam, so *Spitzbuben* will always win. But…' he paused and gave an appreciative nod '…the *Basler brunsli* were very close to my mum's.'

Paige settled back into her seat as the film started to play. 'Perfect,' she said, reaching over in the dimming light to take his hand.

Stefan was touched. Really touched. He still couldn't understand why he'd spoken about his mum earlier, and he'd been glad when Paige hadn't pushed any further.

But this? This was touching. He wished his dad had been here to see what these people he'd known less than a week had done for him. He would have loved this. And he would have loved the chance to sample the cookies.

The warmth from Paige's hand seemed to pulse through his body. All this couldn't be a coincidence. A meeting on a dark road, then in a café, the avalanche, a woman who could match his abilities with her own expertise, and someone with her own demons. There was a connection between them. Maybe it was timing. Maybe it was where they both were in their lives. Maybe it was just physical attraction. But it felt deeper. Paige got him. They were both dancing around each other. She'd revealed some of her demons, and he some of his. Somehow he knew that, like himself, Paige hadn't really done this before. Hadn't told another human being how she was really feeling.

It should be cathartic for them both. But Stefan was uncertain. Paige had said what he might have expected. It wasn't his fault. It helped to hear someone else say that. But he didn't really believe it. Not deep down inside. In a way he almost wished that the road had opened up again, that things could get back to normal and he could fill his life with work.

But Paige had been here when he'd had to stop and think. Admit how guilty he was feeling. And face the demons that had plagued him for the last few years.

Was he using his feelings for Paige to push his guilt into the background? It didn't seem like that. Both things seemed to have hit head-on. But how could he possibly consider any kind of relationship with his work schedule?

It's time to stop, the voice inside his head said. He'd known it was there all along. If

Stefan kept going the way he was, the answer was obvious burn-out. He didn't want that.

But part of what Paige had hinted at really bothered him. She was clearly a great doctor, but a few bad experiences had made her question her career choice. Assault of any healthcare staff was more than criminal, but the fact it had this impact on her made his blood boil.

Paige was arousing every emotion. Desire, protectiveness, lust, curiosity, and maybe a whole lot more.

He just wasn't quite sure what to do next. Despite his workload, his guilt issues, he wanted to let his heart rule his head, ask Paige if she would consider Los Angeles. It would be bold, reckless. It might even be stupid. But as this woman held his hand in the new hospital's cinema, with cookies she'd baked for him, he was sure he was in entirely the right place right now.

This was the place he was supposed to be, and this was the person he was supposed to be with.

He hoped no one would ask him questions about this movie later because, while he was sure it was cute, he couldn't take in a single part of it.

'Hey,' whispered Paige, 'remember your hot chocolate. You need to keep your strength up, you've got sewing to do tonight.'

'We have hours,' he said easily. 'Why do I think you doubt my sewing skills?' His voice was low.

Paige leaned forward. 'Did you hear something?'

He shook his head. 'Hear what?' He took a sip of his hot chocolate and set it on the floor in front of him, listening carefully.

There it was. A muffled shout.

'Guys,' he said in a sharp voice. 'Let's go.'

It was automatic, Cathy, Lynn, Joe and Paige all stood, moving swiftly to the exit. Stefan's mind was on overdrive. The only person missing was Rafe, the Frenchman who'd broken his ribs in the avalanche.

Stefan ran down the corridor to Rafe's room, finding him on the floor next to the bed. He bent down next to him, quickly noticing the wheeze and poor colour.

He opened his mouth to speak, but Paige got in there first. 'He's got a pneumothorax. One of his broken ribs has pierced his lung.' She grabbed a stethoscope from the nearby table and lay on the floor next to Rafe, moving the stethoscope to listen to his chest before giving a nod. 'Right side.'

She turned and rattled off the range of equipment she needed to reinflate his lung. Joe moved instantly to collect the supplies. Cathy wheeled in an ultrasound machine.

Paige and Stefan helped Rafe back up onto the bed, his colour pale, his lips tinged with blue. Stefan slipped some oxygen on him. 'Why did you move? Didn't you press your buzzer?'

Rafe frowned. 'I wa…wanted to get up myself.' He wheezed with every word.

Paige started talking. She was as calm as could be.

'Rafe, one of your broken ribs has punctured your lung. It's collapsed and we need to fix it. This is a relatively simple procedure that I'll be able to do for you. I need you to hold still while I use the ultrasound transducer to find the best place to insert the tube we need to reinflate your lung.'

She moved easily and Stefan could tell that this was a procedure she'd done before. She was confident. She smoothed some gel on the transducer and moved it along the bottom of Rafe's ribs, looking at the screen for the right spot. Stefan recognised it at the same time she did. As she was doing this, she kept her voice steady and calm, talking to Rafe and being completely reassuring.

She marked the spot on his chest wall, then turned to the sterile pack that Joe had found, along with the local anaesthetic. She moved to the sink, washed her hands, and came back to draw up some local anaesthetic into the needle and syringe. 'I'm just going to numb a little area down here,' she said. 'We'll give it a few minutes and then test it again to make sure you can't feel anything.'

Paige expertly cleaned the area, injected the anaesthetic, then went back and washed her hands again, opening the sterile pack and putting some gloves on.

She waited until Rafe's skin area was numb, then took a small scalpel blade. 'You won't feel anything,' she assured him as she made the precise cut. 'You might feel a bit of pressure, or some tugging.'

Stefan watched as Paige slid the tube easily into position, then connected it to the bottle containing water that relieved the pressure on his lung. A few bubbles emerged. Paige moved, and put a few stitches in position to hold the tube. She leaned back and looked at Rafe, smiling. 'Feeling easier?'

Stefan lifted the stethoscope and listened to both lungs again, to check for inflation. Both lungs sounded good.

'Great job.' He smiled as he looked at her, admiring how smoothly she'd dealt with the whole process, from the second she'd entered the room to when she'd placed the final stitches.

She was a great emergency doctor. It would be a tremendous waste if she didn't return to her job. Didn't keep up her skills that could save lives.

Paige continued to take care of Rafe. She used ultrasound to look again and determine that the lung was completely inflated, then adjusted the oxygen supply. She leant next to the bed. 'Now, for the tenth time, I'm going to ask you to stay in bed and not get up unassisted. We will be able to help you move and bring the tube and bottle with you. Please don't get up yourself again.'

Rafe grunted in response. His colour was much better and his oxygen sats were up.

'I'll stay,' offered Cathy. 'I'll give a shout if I need a hand.'

Stefan nodded and gestured to Paige. She looked initially reluctant, but her shoulders relaxed and she gave a smile, packing up the contents of the trolley and clearing it away.

'I have a surprise,' Stefan said in a low voice.

'Oh?' Paige followed him along the corridor. 'Where are we going?'

'Surprise,' he said as he took her into the kitchen and opened the door to a stockroom. He pulled out a bottle of wine.

She let out a little squeal and clapped her hands together a few times. 'Where did you get that?'

'You didn't remember all the alcohol that was in the chalet?'

She groaned. 'Of course, I hadn't really thought about it.' She licked her lips and stared at the bottle. 'This is the part where I hope that this is cheap stuff and nothing vintage, because the truth is, I would never know the difference.'

'You think Baron Boastful would leave good wine at his chalet?'

'I have no idea.' She sighed. 'What if he visits occasionally himself? Maybe he does keep some good stuff there.'

'In that case, I'm sure it would be locked up.' Stefan found a corkscrew and opened the bottle of wine, pouring it into two glasses. 'Here—' he held up his glass '—let's drink to Christmas Eve.'

Paige grinned and held up her own glass. 'What happened to a quiet night and watching a movie?'

She clinked her glass against his. He chose his words carefully. 'You did brilliantly tonight. I was impressed. You didn't even stop to think. You assessed in the blink of an eye, made a decision and started the procedure. Lots of others might have paused, and second-guessed themselves.'

She shook her head. 'Lots of other doctors would be going in blind. I knew his history, had seen his previous X-rays and knew he has broken ribs. It was clear what the fall had done. Anyone could have done it.'

'But *you* did.'

She stared at him for a long moment. The wine glass stilled on her lips. She rested it on the counter again. 'What do you mean?'

He shrugged. 'I'm just stating a fact.'

She shook her head. 'You would have done the same.'

'I'm not sure I would have done it so well, or so quickly.'

Paige waved her hand. 'You're a surgeon. You could manage a chest tube.'

He gave a reluctant nod. 'I could have. But my skills are in other areas. This particular skill was yours.' He paused and then added, 'And you excelled at it.'

Paige's head sagged and she leaned her

elbows on the counter. 'We don't need to do this.'

'We do,' he said determinedly. 'I just watched a brilliant doctor diagnose and treat a patient. Credit where credit is due.'

He could see the struggle written all over her face. Why was he doing this? He knew she was having doubts. But Stefan was struggling too—struggling with the thought that a great doctor was considering throwing her career away and it might just be a blip. One of those moments where a doctor doubted themselves, exhausted by the hours and tasks they'd been doing. He hadn't met a single doctor who hadn't experienced this more than once. He should praise her, he should tell her how good she was. It might be exactly what Paige needed to hear right now and it was all true.

But the slump of her body and head told him this was the last thing she wanted to hear and it actually made his insides ache.

All that training. As soon as that thought appeared in his head he stalled. Maybe this wasn't about Paige. Maybe this was about him? But his life wasn't hers.

His mum and dad had worked like crazy to put him through medical school, with an outcome that no one could have wanted or predicted. He could only imagine the look on their faces if he'd said it had all been for nothing and he was turning his back on his career.

But this wasn't his life, it was Paige's. He'd no idea what her emotional and financial history was. Scottish students got their university education paid for by the state. They still had to take loans to cover accommodation and food, but they certainly had a better deal than some countries.

Paige lifted her head from her hands. The conflict was clear. 'Thank you,' she said softly. 'I've always known I can do the job. What I don't know is if I *want* to do the job.'

She stood up and he knew the night was about to end in a way he didn't want it to. Not like this. Paige was special, through and through.

He stood up next to her and bent over and kissed her forehead. For a moment they stood there, and she wrapped her arms around his waist and buried her head in his shoulder. He could feel her unsteady breathing against his chest. It made him want to hold her all the tighter.

But Paige pulled back. 'I think I need some sleep. Some time to sort things out in my head.' She pressed her lips together for a few seconds, clearly wondering whether to go on. 'Stefan, we could be out of here tomorrow. You live in Los Angeles. I'm in the UK. We've only known each other a few days…' She paused and Stefan broke in.

'None of that matters. I've met you now, Paige McLeod. We're connected. Somehow or other, we're going to be in each other's lives, no matter what else happens. This won't be goodbye. You have some things to work out, and so do I. But the one thing I have worked out is how I feel about you.'

She looked up at him, her dark eyes drinking in every part of him. 'And how's that?'

'You've captured my heart,' he said simply.

It was everything. He was putting himself on the line for someone in the middle of a career crisis, and in the midst of an emergency situation. If he'd been counselling a friend about this situation, he'd likely have warned them against making any big declarations until they were back home and ready to breathe again.

But this just felt right. He had to say it. He had to be honest. The thought of not seeing, speaking or touching Paige again was already alien to him. And maybe he was calling this all wrong. Now was the time to find out.

She blinked, her eyes shining with unshed tears. The edges of her lips turned upwards and she gave him a soft smile. 'I feel the same,' she admitted. 'This was the last thing I was expecting, but it feels like…' her brow wrinkled as she thought, but she gave a shake of her head and met his gaze again '…it was meant to be. I've never been so connected with someone before. I don't know what will happen next. I guess we just need to find out.'

He kissed her head again, as his heart swelled in his chest. It was everything he wanted to hear, and in another time and place they would have headed straight for the nearest room.

And they would. But Stefan knew tonight that Paige needed some space. And he would absolutely give her whatever she needed.

'I'll be next door,' he said gently. 'If you want a hug, just come on in.'

She reached up and traced a finger down the side of his face. 'Thank you,' she whispered.

'Always,' he replied, and put his arm around her shoulder as they walked along the corridor, and back to the suite.

CHAPTER EIGHT

CHRISTMAS MORNING WAS still dark. But Lynn had managed to get up early, string up some more Christmas lights and link up her phone to play some background music. Paige awoke to the smell of coffee and bacon drifting down the corridor towards her, as she was swamped by the snuggly duvet.

Her first thoughts were for Stefan. He wasn't next to her, and she hadn't climbed into his bed last night. Maybe she should have. But the space had let her make the decision that had been playing in her mind for a while. She hadn't told a soul. But it was as if a huge weight had been lifted off her shoulders.

She was going to take some more time off. She would reassess her specialty, explore her options and decide if she wanted to stay in any part of medicine. She wasn't sure right now what the outcome would be. But she was comfortable with her decision.

The tiny knot that had been in her stomach for as long as she could remember was gone. She would let Leo know as soon as possible, though she suspected he might have already known this was on the cards.

Maybe she would visit Los Angeles? Maybe she would consider a career in another country. All she knew was that she was free to explore that option.

She glanced at the time. It was six a.m. Stefan was obviously up before her as the other room was empty. She wondered if he'd helped with the extra decorations. As she approached the kitchen she realised she was the last one up. The others were sitting having breakfast and whispering to each other.

Cathy gave her a broad smile and put a finger to her lips. 'We don't want to wake Claudia too early.'

'Is everything ready for her?'

The rest all nodded. 'It might not be what she put on her original Santa list, but at least she'll get some presents.'

Joe slid some bacon onto a plate alongside some toast and pushed the plate towards her. 'Wait until you see her stocking. It's a masterpiece.'

She turned to face Stefan. She'd totally forgotten that he'd still had the stocking to stitch last night. Had there been any chance for him to sleep at all?

'What did you do?' she asked with a smile on her face.

He tapped the side of his nose. 'Just wait and see. I bet Claudia will be up soon.'

Now she was intrigued. Paige ate the bacon sandwich she put together and sipped the coffee. Apart from the timing, this was pretty much how she would have spent Christmas morning if she'd been on her own. She might not have got dressed, but her comfortable jeans and T-shirt weren't too big an ask.

'What about the rest of today? Do you need me to do anything?'

Stefan shook his head and looked at Joe. 'We've got it all under control, haven't we?'

Joe nodded in agreement. 'You guys can go and spend time with our patients and leave us to it. Christmas dinner should be ready around three.'

Lynn pulled over a round biscuit tin. 'I put all the extra cookies from last night in here. So there's plenty of nibbles for people.'

'Has anyone checked on Rafe yet?'

Cathy smiled. 'He was fine overnight. I'll

leave the check this morning to you. We've got a wheelchair, so he'll be able to come through and eat Christmas dinner with everyone else.'

Stefan asked the one question everyone had avoided so far. 'What about the weather?'

Joe held up the satellite phone. 'They might have a small window around four p.m., and later around six p.m. Franco asked if we had any objection if some of the people from the café were picked up first.'

Stefan frowned. 'Rafe should really be the priority. Are there issues down at the café we should know about?'

Joe held up his hands. 'There are fourteen children down at the café. I think Franco is anxious to try and get them back to their families. Only two of them have parents with them. The rest are with school teachers and were on a school outing.'

Paige nodded. 'That's hard. I can't imagine how upset some of them must have been—their parents too. Is it wrong to let them go first?' She cleared her throat. 'Let me assess Rafe this morning. If I have any concerns I'll let you know. If I think he's stable, I think we should consider Franco's request. Sorry, folks.'

They all nodded. There was a shout from along the corridor. 'Santa's been!' The delight in Claudia's voice was clear.

They all made their way down to Claudia and Marie's room, Stefan putting his arm around Paige's waist as they went. 'Good morning,' he whispered, planting a kiss on her cheek.

'Good morning,' she replied, wishing they were alone.

As they rounded the corner into Claudia's room, Paige's eyes went wide.

The red and green Christmas stocking was bigger than normal—clearly designed to hold all the presents they'd managed to pull together. There was a jigsaw, some chocolate, colouring books and pens, even a small teddy bear. Paige was going to have to email the Baron about all the missing items from the chalet. But the look on Claudia's face right now was worth it.

'Mummy,' she said in amazement, 'this stocking has my name on it. Can I keep it?'

Marie nodded, her eyes filled with tears. *Thank you*, she mouthed to them all.

Paige moved a little closer, looking at the detail on the stocking. It was stitched together from felt, then had smaller pieces of felt cut into a variety of designs and stitched at various points on the stocking. There was a Santa, a Christmas tree, presents and something special. Claudia had just spotted it too.

'Look, Mummy, it's a little bird, like the one in the window at the front doors.'

Sure enough, in multiple colours, Stefan had stitched a little Turaco bird into the design of the stocking.

Paige moved back over to Stefan. 'That's beautiful. I can't believe you had time to do all this. It must have taken hours.'

He shrugged. 'Look at her. It's worth it. This hasn't been the Christmas any of us expected. Here's hoping we can all get out of here later.'

Paige swallowed, realising that she didn't actually have anywhere to go. She could go home, of course, back to the UK. She was supposed to be staying here, still in the chalet. But if the road was going to take days, or even weeks, to clear she would have to be evacuated with everyone else.

'What about your father?' she asked Stefan.

A line creased his brow. 'I haven't been able to contact him yet. It's still early.'

'He'll be disappointed that you won't get home today,' she said sympathetically.

'Maybe. But he'll understand. It will be more important to him that I'm somewhere I can be helping people.'

It was the right thing to say. Paige knew that. But it just didn't feel right.

'Really?' she asked. 'Your father would rather you were working than spend time with you at Christmas?'

When his gaze met hers his expression was guarded, something else lurking just behind the surface. She knew she should delve more deeply.

But this was Christmas Day. It wasn't the right time. A little voice sounded in her head. Would they have more Christmases together after this one? She certainly hoped so.

It was odd. She just felt so much lighter. Her decision was made and she would live with the repercussions. She would tell Stefan later, when they had some time to themselves.

He blinked again, still looking at her. 'My dad always wants what's best for me, and for others. My parents always put themselves last.'

Paige wondered if it was supposed to sound self-sacrificing, and maybe it was, but it just sounded ultimately sad to her and, from the expression on Stefan's face, to him too.

He lifted his head. 'I have dinner to prepare.' It was as if someone had flicked a switch because all of a sudden he had a broad smile on his face and he was reaching for Joe to encourage him to start helping.

Paige wanted to offer to help too. To encourage Stefan to talk. To ask if he'd ever sat down with his dad and told him how guilty he felt about his mum. But she knew that had never happened. She also knew that Stefan was working himself to death to avoid that conversation. Something really had to give.

She walked down the corridor to check on Rafe. He was looking better and eating a large bowl of porridge that Lynn had made for him. She checked the level in the bottle and listened to his chest again.

She sat on the edge of the bed—against all the rules—and spoke to him. 'There is a small chance that, later on today, we might get a chance to evacuate by helicopter.'

Rafe immediately stopped eating. He glanced at the tube coming out of his chest. 'But how can I be moved with this? Does it mean I can't go?'

She shook her head. 'No, it doesn't mean that. You're stable. We would consider you fit to transfer. It does mean we have to be extra careful. The bottle must be kept upright, and it has to be below the level of your chest. We would strap you into a special stretcher and have the bottle and tube protected and strapped against you for the transfer.'

For a moment he breathed a sigh of relief, and then looked worried again. 'When could this be?'

'Around six p.m. tonight. Long after Christmas dinner—Stefan and Joe are not getting out of that one.' She gave a laugh, and then paused. 'They might be able to get some people out earlier. But there are fourteen children down at the café—some of them with no parents. Franco asked if they could be evacuated first.'

'Absolutely,' said Rafe without a moment's hesitation and a half-shrug. 'After all, where am I going to go? Just to another hospital that's down the valley. My family is back in France. I expect it will be a few weeks before I take a flight back home. Let the kids go first and hopefully some will get to see their families today.'

Paige gave a smile and patted his arm. 'I was hoping you would say that.' She gave him an amused look. 'From the man who didn't want to stay in his bed at all, you've changed your tune.'

He tapped his ribs. 'I've learned to pace myself. I want to get back out and ski. I need to let these ribs heal, and I know I put myself back by having the fall. What can I say? Lesson learned.'

She sighed. 'If only all patients were so obliging.'

He gave her a look of admiration. 'People should be grateful that you're their doctor and listen to you. I'm grateful. You knew exactly what you were doing and didn't hesitate. Thank you.'

She felt a pang in her chest. Moments like this were few and far between. It felt as if people had stopped saying thank you in the health service. Life seemed full of complaints and investigations.

'Thank you,' she said as she stood up. 'It's appreciated.'

He gave a nod and she walked back down the corridor, taking a few moments to go back to the suite she shared with Stefan.

The day was still dark. They might get evacuated—they might not. She certainly wouldn't be able to take the suitcase of belongings she'd brought to Switzerland with her. She would have to get it sent on at a later date.

Paige didn't want to be short of time, so she folded up some clothes, alongside her passport and personal belongings, and put them in a small holdall. She would be ready to go at short notice if needed.

She changed her T-shirt and freshened up her hair and make-up before going back along to the main room. There was a competitive game of Monopoly about to start and she joined in, familiarising herself with the Switzerland equivalent of Mayfair.

The atmosphere was cheerful. People knew there was at least half a chance of getting home later. That, and because the day they had all dreaded being here had actually arrived, made things feel much better. Again, she was grateful to be somewhere safe. Somewhere warm, and with people she now considered friends.

She brought along a pot of coffee and put the extra cookies on plates, and they were soon gone. It didn't take long for wonderful smells to drift down the corridor towards them. She could hear raucous laughter coming from the kitchen, mainly from Joe and his stories. Lynn rolled her eyes. 'He's got new blood for telling all his operating theatre tales. He'll be in his element today.' She leaned forward. 'Let's just hope he doesn't put Stefan off the food.'

The afternoon continued to be dark and gloomy, but the mood in the hospital was jubilant and light. Every now and then Paige would notice someone get a little quieter, or spend a few moments on their own, and that was fine. Christmas was a time for families, and these were exceptional circumstances, all were entitled to their own thoughts.

Joe came along with a whoop of celebration. 'Food is ready, people. Take your places.'

Paige positioned Rafe at the table, the bottle at the side of his wheelchair, and the others took their chairs at the long table.

Cathy, Lynn and Paige went down to the kitchen to help carry the food along, and found themselves bringing trays of potato salad and vegetables. Joe and Stefan followed with silver platters of *filet em tieg* and *shinkli em tieg*. The pastry-wrapped delights smelled delicious. 'I can't wait to try these,' Paige said with a smile as she took one of each and passed the platter down the table.

The dinner was a success, the food delicious. The only thing they didn't do was drink any wine—not if there was a chance of transport later in the evening. Paige offered to wash the dishes, conscious that if they were evacuated she didn't want to leave any mess in the hospital.

Stefan joined her as she loaded the dishwasher and filled the sink for some of the larger pots. He seemed distracted but slipped his arms around her as he finished drying one of the pots.

'When the helicopter comes,' he said slowly, 'will you come with me?'

She held her breath, turning around to look at him. 'Why?'

He was clearly confused by the question. 'Because I thought you wouldn't have somewhere to go. I want to spend more time with you. I'd like you to meet my father.'

She reached and touched his cheek. 'I would love to meet your father, and I would love to spend more time with you. But you have to be ready for that.'

He blinked and pulled back. 'What do you mean?'

She brought down her hand and started knotting the dish towel she'd just used to dry dishes between her two hands. 'I mean, I made a decision this morning. I'm not going to be a doctor any more. Not in A&E at least. Maybe not at all. I still need to figure out that part. I can't keep doing a job that's making me miserable.' She lifted her hand to her heart. 'But until I'd sorted this part of me, and this part of me—' she pointed to her head '—I wasn't going to have room to commit to something new, something different.'

She could see him trying to connect the dots in his jumbled brain. 'You're telling me you couldn't consider starting a relationship until you'd decided to give up your job? That's madness. It doesn't even make sense.'

Paige took a deep breath. 'But it does, for me. And there's something you need to do too.'

He shook his head. 'You've lost me now.'

'Why are you so busy all the time? Why do you plan your life without a moment to spare? Because I know it's deliberate. But do you know it is?'

He stood frozen to the spot for a few minutes. 'I'm busy because, unlike you, I love my work. I want to be busy. I thrive on being busy. I want to do as much as I can to help as many people as possible.'

Paige stepped forward and put one finger on his chest. She wasn't annoyed by the earlier jibe. It had hardly even registered. 'But when do you stop to help yourself?'

She was barely inches from his face. Confusion crossed his face. But only for a moment. Because Stefan did know what she was talking about. He did understand. But was he ready to confront his demons?

'This is ridiculous.' His jaw was tight. 'All I want to do is ask you to come back with me. Ask you to come and meet my father.'

Her hand reached out and touched his. 'And I would love to do that. But I don't want to get in the way of the conversation you need to have with your father.'

'What?'

He was still in denial and, before she had a chance to say anything more, he swung the conversation around. 'And what about you? Aren't you being hasty? After all those years of training, you're prepared to walk away? I mean, I get what happened to you in A&E is totally unacceptable. But you said your boss was making changes and bringing in security—won't that make things better?'

Paige took a deep breath. 'Maybe for others, but not for me.'

'If you don't want to go back there, you could be a doctor anywhere. What about Los Angeles? Why don't you come back with me—take some time to get to know the place, then decide where you'd like to work? There will be plenty of job opportunities for someone with your experience. You could pick and choose.'

'But what if I'm choosing not to be a doctor? Would I still be welcome to join you in Los Angeles?' Her words were sharp, she knew that. But she was getting exasperated. She was getting jittery. In a short period of time, she might find herself hoisted up into a helicopter. It wasn't exactly filling her thoughts with confidence.

And Stefan just didn't seem to be listening. He wasn't acknowledging the fact that Paige could see right through him. That whilst she might have met a wonderful man who made her heart sing, she had to be sure about what she did next.

And that included being sure about him.

She took a deep breath. 'When are you going to realise you can't keep going on like this? Have you ever sat down with your dad and spoken about your mum? Have you told him how guilty you feel? Have you told him you didn't realise how sick she was and that you wish you could have done something to intervene?'

Stefan pulled right back from her, as if she'd wounded him with her words. But these words weren't harsh. They were just the truth.

'This isn't any of your business.'

She froze. 'You're absolutely right, they're not. But I'd like it to be my business. You just asked me to go to Los Angeles with you. You're inviting me to fly halfway around the world with you. But you're also telling me I can't tell you what I'm seeing, and what I think you need to do. What happens if I come to Los Angeles? Will I ever see you? Or will you continue to work—what is it?—fourteen hours a day, seven days a week? I want to take a chance. But I want to take a chance on *us*, Stefan. If you keep going like you are now, there will never be a chance for an *us*. Can't you see that?'

He walked away, shaking his head, and Paige crossed her hands in front of her heart. She said the words that he really needed to understand—because if he didn't there could never be any chance for them.

'There isn't room for me to love you, Stefan, until you learn to love yourself first.'

And, even though there were tears in her eyes, she turned and walked out.

CHAPTER NINE

THE PAIN STARTED in his chest with every breath. His hands were shaking, and he couldn't get them to stop.

He knew exactly what Paige was saying to him. He just didn't ever want to stop and have that conversation with his father.

He hated that so much of what she'd said was right. He'd been tired lately—exhausted, even—sometimes functioning on four hours' sleep a night. His diary was a whirlwind of dates, surgeries and venues. He consciously said yes to just about everything, juggling dates so he could fit all requests in.

He pulled out his phone and stared at it. He was going to check something but, deep down, knew the answer wasn't something he really wanted to find.

He scrolled. In the last five years he'd had thirty-five days off. One week a year. He'd generally gone skiing somewhere for a few days or seen his father, but that had been it. No down time. Even when he was travelling between countries he was still working. No wonder she was calling him out.

He could picture his father's face right now. His chest tightened at the thought of bringing up the subject of his mother. What on earth would he do if he found out that his father also blamed him for his mother's death? That was secretly what he feared. His father had been totally devoted to her. He knew that he missed her terribly—just like Stefan did.

There were voices down the corridor, movement, excitement.

Joe was talking loudly on the satellite phone, taking instructions from Paige.

He looked outside. Paige's hair was swept up in a ponytail, she had her outdoor clothes on, and a holdall on her back. She was on her knees, securing Rafe's chest drain bottle.

'Is the helicopter on its way?' he asked, striding down the corridor.

Cathy appeared behind him, pushing another wheelchair with Claudia, and her mother walking alongside.

'There's still a limited timeframe. We're

going to try and get Rafe and Claudia airlifted at the same time.'

Stefan could see it was still windy outside. The helicopter would have to drop the stretcher then hoist it back up. It would be dangerous for all involved.

'What's the estimated arrival time?'

'Five minutes.' Paige's voice was calm and professional. She didn't even look in his direction. All her attention was focused on her current patient. She spoke again. 'Stefan, go and assess everyone else for the order in which they'll be evacuated. The helicopter will try and make return trips, but it might not be possible.'

He wanted to talk to her again. But this wasn't the time.

He moved to check over Bob, Frances, Eva, Anna and Greta, helping them into outdoor jackets and giving them a rundown of what could happen next.

The thudding of the helicopter rotors cut through the wind noise. A few moments later, there was an icy blast down the corridor as the front doors were opened.

Stefan pulled the two chairs with the ladies with broken ankles as Bob and Eva walked behind.

The helicopter was hovering over the car

park area of the hospital. With trees surrounding the car park, it wasn't a safe place to land but, as Stefan watched, the side door slid open and the stretcher was winched down. Joe and Paige were with Rafe; Joe had the satellite phone between his ear and shoulder.

They wrestled Rafe into the stretcher, positioning his bottle and giving the signal for him to go up. As he lifted up to the helicopter, Joe handed the phone to Paige. The noise from the rotor blades was enormous, Stefan had no idea how on earth Paige could hear anything. But a few minutes later a harness descended, she clipped herself in, put her holdall on her back and, before he knew it, was lifted into the sky.

A sense of dread swept over him. They hadn't had a chance to talk yet. He hadn't told her how sorry he was, and how he'd been too wrapped up in himself to truly understand and appreciate how she was feeling.

The stretcher for Claudia came back down as Stefan ran over to help Joe. The little girl was much easier to manoeuvre and get clipped in. 'What's going on?' Stefan asked Joe as the winch lifted Claudia into the air.

'The doctor on board isn't feeling well.

Asked if someone could help with the transfer.' The wind and backdraught were playing havoc with having any kind of discussion. The harness descended again and they clipped Marie, Claudia's mother, in. She lifted into the sky easily and, as she was assisted in, the door slid closed.

Before Stefan had a chance to think, or say anything at all, the dark helicopter moved off, disappearing into the distance.

Joe put his hand on his shoulder, oblivious to what had just happened between Stefan and Paige. 'They hope to get back in thirty minutes. They can get the rest of our people out then, and will come back for us if there's time.'

His stomach flipped over. He couldn't help but think he'd made a huge mistake in not taking the time to sit down with Paige and talk again.

Stefan swallowed. He had no idea where the helicopter was going. Likely it would be one of the bigger hospitals in the nearby city. Would Paige wait there? Or would she leave?

Deep down, he knew the answer to that.

And, what was more, he deserved it.

CHAPTER TEN

LEO GAVE HER a huge hug as he presented her with a bunch of flowers and gift cards from her colleagues in the department. 'I'll miss you,' he said. 'But I know you're doing what's right for you. Any letter of recommendation you want, just let me know.'

Paige was holding back the tears. Some of her colleagues had been shocked, others not so much. When she'd handed in her resignation Leo had hung his head for a few seconds, then took a deep breath and talked everything through with her. She'd worked her notice, finishing early as she still had holidays owed, and had put some of her things in storage as she planned to go travelling.

Her mum and dad had been stunned, and maybe a little disappointed. But when she'd told them how she'd been feeling about work they'd accepted her decision. She knew that they both hoped that all she needed was a break. Paige was lucky. She had some savings and knew that she would be fine for a few months.

Her stomach gave a little twist and she did the thing she'd been doing for the last few weeks—tried not to think about Stefan. She knew she'd made the right decision about her work life, but had she made the right decision about her personal life? She hated how things had been left, and that even the thought of travelling brought up instant memories of that gorgeous Swiss chalet and the one night she'd spent there in his arms.

Paige sighed as she emptied her locker, put away her scrubs and changed into her jeans and T-shirt. There was a small pang as she closed her locker for the last time and walked out through the front doors of A&E.

Her steps were lighter, and automatically took her over to her favourite café. She smiled as she sat in the bench seat and ordered the specials of the day. Hot chocolate with marshmallows, flake and cream, and some apple tart. She could smell it already and she couldn't help but smile.

There was a creak, and someone slid

into the seat opposite. She blinked. No. It couldn't be.

'Hey,' Stefan said softly. 'Long time no see.'

'Sixteen days,' she said without a blink of her eyes.

He licked his lips. 'I'm sorry.'

She pressed her lips together and tried to ignore the rapid beating of her heart. 'I don't need you to be sorry. I need you to tell me what you've done.'

He took a deep breath. 'I spoke to my father.'

'You did?' Her stomach clenched tightly.

He nodded.

'How did it go?' Part of her was dreading the answer.

He bit his bottom lip. 'It probably went as expected. He said my mother was stubborn and he'd told her to see a doctor and she'd refused. The money was a huge aspect for them, and they were both anxious to support me as best they could.' He sighed. 'He doesn't think my mother would have listened to me either.'

She gave a small nod. 'Did you tell him how you felt?'

That had clearly been tougher for him. He closed his eyes for a second. 'I told him I felt responsible. I told him I felt guilty I hadn't been around more to help and give her advice on her health.'

'And what did he say?'

Stefan lifted his head and looked her in the eye. 'He told me he felt guilty too. He should have noticed. He should have stopped her. He said he had no excuse, since he saw her every day.'

'Wow…' Paige leaned back in her seat. 'That's huge.'

Stefan nodded. 'We both felt guilty, and never told each other. He asked me about work, and I told him about you instead.'

'You did?' The tiny hairs on her arms stood on end.

'I did. He was amused, you know.'

Her brow furrowed. 'Why?'

'Because apparently I've never spoken about anyone the way I spoke about you. It reminded him of the way he used to speak about Mum.'

She wasn't quite sure what to say.

'Apparently all I've ever done is talk about my next piece of work. He asked me if I planned to slow down.'

Her skin prickled again. The words caught in her throat. 'What are your plans?'

He smiled. 'It might surprise you to hear

I've taken some time off. All surgeries have been rescheduled. The road has been cleared in Switzerland and is getting repaired. We have another project manager, who is taking over the last of the renovations.'

Paige gave a nod towards her flowers. 'And I take it you know that I've just worked my last day?'

The waitress appeared and put two large hot chocolates and two pieces of pie on the table. 'Thought I might as well bring two,' she said brightly.

Stefan gave a nervous smile.

'You've actually taken time off?'

He nodded.

'And what are your plans?'

His hands closed around the hot chocolate glass. 'I have one tiny thing I want to do, but then I was hoping we could make plans together.'

Her breathing caught somewhere in the back of her throat. The second he'd sat down she'd just wanted to hug him, to kiss him. Each of the sixteen days they'd been apart she'd been haunted by doubts—wondering if she'd done the right thing by calling him out and walking away. The temptation to wait for him when she'd stepped off the helicopter and seen her patients to safety had been overwhelming. But the place had been chaos, and it had been easy to slip through the waiting people with her small holdall and find a hotel for the night.

He'd phoned her, texted, but she'd known that they both had things to take care of.

'I'm not sure I want to be a doctor at all,' she said, her voice wavering. 'I need time to find out what is right. And I need the person I'm with to support me, to have my back.'

He reached his hands across the table and took hers. 'I promise I will support whatever you want to do. I'm sorry I tried to push you into staying. I was projecting my feelings and emotions into your situation and I should never have done that. Whatever you want to do, wherever you want to do it—I've got your back.'

She raised her eyes to meet his. 'And if I want to do it in Los Angeles?'

His face broke into a wide smile. 'Then I'd be honoured if you stay with me while you work things out.'

'No pressure?' she reiterated.

'No pressure,' he said in a reassuring voice. 'Just someone who loves you and wants you to be happy.'

Paige breathed. It was like being back in the Alps and breathing in clean mountain air. Then she twigged what he'd mentioned earlier. 'You said something else—you said you had something to do first. What's that?'

For the first time since she'd known him Stefan looked a little sheepish. 'Yeah, about that. You know how I told you I'd spoken to my father?'

She nodded.

'Well, he was quite insistent about one thing.'

'What was that?'

'That he got to meet the woman who'd captured my heart.'

He nodded behind her, and Paige turned around. There was an older man sitting a few booths behind her, drinking coffee and eating apple pie. He lifted his filled fork towards her with a wide grin, and gave a nod.

Paige's mouth fell open. 'You didn't?'

Stefan smiled. 'He was pretty insistent and, to be honest, having the two people I love most in the world meet each other seemed like a good idea.'

Paige let out a squeal of delight and jumped up, leaning over the table and grabbing Stefan in a huge hug. 'I'd be delighted to meet your dad!'

Stefan started laughing and stood up, then slipped his hand into hers. 'He's going to love you,' he whispered in her ear. 'Just as much as I do.'

Paige smiled and leaned into his kiss, for now and always.

EPILOGUE

THE ROAD WAS in perfect order as they drove up towards the hospital. 'I can't believe it's a year since it opened,' said Paige, staring out of the window at the snow-capped mountains.

Stefan reached a warm hand over and squeezed her knee. 'I never thought I'd be grateful to an avalanche.'

Paige met his gaze for a second and slipped her hand over his. 'It's so weird being back. I'm not sure whether I prefer the sun in Los Angeles or the air in the Alps.'

'Don't let my dad hear you saying that,' Stefan joked.

They turned the final corner, pulling into the large, landscaped car park that now had a helipad at one end.

The hospital looked even better than the last time they'd been here. New windows had been put into the older building, and

Paige could see the state-of-the-art gym. The whole building was finished in a pale cream colour, but the main door remained the same with its stained-glass panels on either side.

'How many patients do you have?' asked Paige.

'Seven,' Stefan replied with a smile. 'Two toddlers for cleft repairs, and five adults, some reconstruction surgery after treatment, a skin graft, and some nose and cheek surgeries.'

The car came to a halt in one of the spaces and they stepped out into the crisp fresh air. 'Any time to ski?' asked Paige, teasing.

'Maybe a little,' he said, slipping an arm around her waist as they walked to the main doors. 'But we have to fit that in between meeting my father for dinner one evening, and Franco the next.'

'I'm sure we'll manage,' she said, putting her head on his shoulder. As they walked up the steps, she looked at him curiously. 'What is it you wanted to show me?'

He tapped the side of his nose. 'Let's say our hellos first.'

They greeted the nursing and theatre staff, general manager, chef and domestic staff. Discretion was key at the alpine hospital.

All the staff were professional but the atmosphere was relaxed and easy.

Stefan slipped his hand into Paige's and led her down the corridor to the room that doubled as his office. As they walked in, he gestured for her to sit down.

There was a long white box on the table and Paige smiled, wondering what on earth was going on.

Instead of walking around to the other side of the desk, he pulled over another chair from the wall and sat down next to her. 'I got you a gift.' He smiled, nodding at the box. 'Open it.'

She gave him a curious smile. 'Okay.' She shifted position and lifted the lid of the white box. Inside was a carved wooden plaque. At one end was a brightly coloured Turaco bird, but it was the name and title that caught her attention. She ran her finger along the letters: *Paige McLeod, Counsellor.*

'It's beautiful,' she breathed, one hand going up to her chest.

'I know it's early. But once you qualify, your office will be next to mine. Here, and in Los Angeles.' He waved his hand to the room next door, which was identical to his, only a little smaller.

She couldn't hide the tears in her eyes.

He'd supported her every step of the way, just like he'd promised. 'I love the bird. Signifying where we met.' She met his blue eyes. 'Where we fell in love.'

He cleared his throat. 'There's another door plaque underneath.'

She tilted her head to the side, wondering what on earth he meant. 'Why would I need another?'

She lifted the first and looked underneath. There was an identical plaque, with the Turaco bird and a name—only this time it read *Paige Bachmann, Counsellor.*

Her hand went to her mouth and her head turned quickly. Stefan was kneeling on the floor, an open ring box in his hand. 'What do you think?' He smiled. 'And you can have whatever name you like—the question is still the same—will you marry me?'

'Yes!' There wasn't a single moment's hesitation in her answer as she wrapped her arms around his neck, laughing and kissing him.

'Aren't I supposed to put the ring on your finger?' He laughed as she almost knocked him over.

She held out her trembling hand so he could slide the single pink diamond onto her finger. 'One thing,' she whispered.

'Anything,' he said immediately.

She raised her eyebrows. 'I get the bigger office.'

'Mrs Bachmann,' he agreed, 'can have whatever she wants.' And he picked her up and swung her around as they both laughed.

* * * * *

If you enjoyed this story, check out these other great reads from Scarlet Wilson

Neonatal Doc on Her Doorstep
The Night They Never Forgot
Marriage Miracle in Emergency
A Festive Fling in Stockholm

All available now!